Thomas Jefferson Jerome

Ku-Klux Klan No. 40

A Novel

Thomas Jefferson Jerome

Ku-Klux Klan No. 40
A Novel

ISBN/EAN: 9783337032166

Printed in Europe, USA, Canada, Australia, Japan

Cover: Foto ©Andreas Hilbeck / pixelio.de

More available books at **www.hansebooks.com**

KU-KLUX KLAN No. 40.

A NOVEL.

By Thomas J. Jerome.

———————

RALEIGH, N. C.:
EDWARDS & BROUGHTON, PRINTERS AND BINDERS.
1895.

PREFACE.

Ku-Kluxism is dead, and I have no desire to re-open the wounds inflicted by its bloody hands. I would to God that the very recollection of the existence of such an organization could be lost, and that all record of its deeds could be effaced.

"Secret political societies are dangerous to the liberties of a free people, and should not be tolerated."— Constitution of North Carolina (1875).

But while the hand of Ku-Kluxism is stained with blood, yet, considering the sufferings the South endured during the brief existence of that organization, it is the purest and whitest hand ever raised by an outraged people to repel the assaults of their oppressors. Under the reconstruction laws of Congress the people of the South were required to overthrow their own State governments; to repudiate, not only their State debts, but their own private contracts, as well; to ratify the taking from them by force, and without remuneration, almost their entire property, and to adopt Constitutions for their government which stripped them of the right dearest to every citizen—the right to vote and hold office, while the ignorant black man was clothed with all the rights and immunities of citizenship. Is it any wonder, then, that the people took refuge in Ku-Klux Klans, that they might strike against the ruin and desolation, peculation and violence that threatened to destroy them? When Federal bayonets were used to enforce the intolerable exactions of the government in the way of taxes, and the arm of the negro militia to sustain black demons in their violation of the sanctity of homes and the chastity of women—is it any wonder that men rushed into secret societies for the defense of their wives, their mothers, their sisters and their homes?

Long before a Ku-Klux was ever heard of in the South, armed mobs of negroes and low-down scalawags and carpet-baggers were marching through our towns and country, insulting citizens and spreading terror among all classes. Carpet-bag judges so interpreted the law that scalawag juries found it an easy task to acquit these demons when charged with crime; but if, perchance, a conviction could be had, a Republican Governor stood ready to pardon the offender for his vote. The result was that all good men were alarmed for the safety of their property and families, and they very naturally looked for some measures of protection.

But the cloud that overshadowed the South has vanished, and the sunlight of peace and prosperity now lights up every pathway. Hope has returned, and the statue of liberty has thrown its torch into every corner. Life, liberty and property are as safe in the South to-day as anywhere on the globe, and while the acquisition of power by the better element may not fully pardon the method of obtaining it, yet justice will declare that the use of this power by the better classes in building up the country clearly vindicates their right to it.

Nearly all the scenes described in this book are founded on well authenticated historical facts. The pictures here given have been gathered from the histories of the Southern States, and a truthfulness of portraiture is the only merit claimed for the work. Born in October, 1859, I was too young to take any part in the operations of the Ku-Klux, or to know much of their actions, except what I have learned from history. So far as I know, no relation of mine ever belonged to the Klan, though my father was deprived, for some time, of his right to vote by the Federal authorities—an indignity his son will never forget.

THE AUTHOR.

Albemarle, N. C., 1895.

CONTENTS.

KU-KLUX KLAN No. 40.

CHAPTER I.

"Klan No. 40!"

"A white man's government!"

"Death to scallawags, carpet-baggers and niggers!"

Such were the exclamations of a tall and athletic young man, as he entered the almost impenetrable woods at the foot of Glen Echo.

He was a Ku-Klux, and the first exclamation given above [simply announced the number of the den to which he belonged; the second, the annual password, and the third, the universal motto of the Klan respecting political matters.

The hills around Glen Echo were covered with tall and stately oaks and poplars, and a dense undergrowth of laurel, and under this shadowy foliage the young man secreted himself. He was reclining quietly on a bed of leaves, when the pensive tranquility of the evening was disturbed by the sound of horses' feet on the road crossing at the foot of the glen. Raising himself on his elbow, he peered through the laurel to discover who the intruders were.

The first glimpse of the riders brought the young man to his feet, with a flush of indignation on his cheek and a scowl of dissatisfaction on his brow. Shaking his clenched fist at the male intruder, for the equestrians were in fact a young man and young lady taking an evening ride, he muttered between his teeth :

"You miserable South-hating carpet-bagger! How dare you come in here and try to usurp my place in the affection of that girl, whom you know I love ; that her father despises you, and that I hate you? I swear by all the energies of my soul I will yet win her, and save her the offense of marrying a radical carpet-bagger if, in order to do so, I shall have to dip my finger in your heart's blood, and write K. K. K. on the lid of your coffin !"

This ominous threat was not heard by either of the riders. On the contrary, they stopped their horses within a few feet of the young man in the thicket, and the gentleman on horseback plucked a sprig of laurel and handed it to the young lady, who placed the stem in her bosom, and then, plucking a tiny twig containing only two leaves, she leaned forward in her saddle and pinned the leaves to the lappel of the young man's coat.

During this time the young man in the laurel bushes was compelled, much to his discomfiture, to listen to the following conversation :

"I have been thinking, Minnie," said the young man on horseback, addressing the young lady in tones which indicated the deepest passion, "that the condition to our union which you impose makes it utterly impossible for us to ever consummate our wishes in marriage. You know your father's aversion for a carpet-bagger, and you know he refuses to recognize me by any other name, or to see in me anything but the infamy and disgrace which such an appellation implies; and I fear that your promise to marry me only on condition that

I first obtain your father's consent, is to place an insurmountable barrier betwixt us, and one that will remain there forever."

The earnest but despairing tones of the speaker caused the young lady to sigh deeply, but still she answered firmly :

"You must be convinced, Judge Farwell, from my promise to marry you at all, though the promise be coupled with the condition of which you complain, that I cherish for you an affection which makes our marriage necessary to my own happiness as well as, I hope, to yours; but I should have to consider myself very remiss in filial duty to take upon myself such a fearful responsibility without the consent of my father."

"Excuse me for pleading with you," answered Judge Farwell, "and now, if you will allow me to retaliate, I will promise you never to mention this part of our subject again, on one condition : that is, if you will answer me one question, the answer to which I am anxious to know."

"I suppose I might allow you to ask your question," said the young lady.

"But you might consider it a silly one."

"Then I would advise you not to ask it. I have never known you to do a silly thing, and I would be sorry to have you detract from your reputation in that respect."

"But jealousy demands it, and I must ask it even at the risk of being considered foolish. I want to know if you love John Latham?"

"There was no necessity for such a question, and I am surprised at it," answered the young lady. "Indeed,

I am tempted to refuse an answer, not simply because I think it a silly question, but because I consider it a reflection upon my honesty. It seems to me you give me little credit for sincerity if you think I would promise to marry you while loving another."

"Oh, I did not mean to question your sincerity in the least, I assure you," answered the judge, "but you know jealousy is the torment of every newly-accepted lover, and knowing how popular you have been in the town, and how assiduous Mr. Latham has been in his attentions to you, I could not keep the monster out of my heart."

"Then if you really consider yourself entitled to an answer, I will give it," answered the young lady: "Mr. Latham and I have been reared children together, and I have always esteemed him a very true friend, but I have never thought of him as a lover, and I do not know that he has ever wished me to so regard him. He has my sincerest friendship and utmost confidence; nothing more."

"That was very kindly spoken," answered the judge, "and with [this assurance I will banish the monster from my breast, and trusting you as implicitly as I would have you trust me, I will content myself with the hope that the rancor of party spirit will soon subside in our community, and that the inveterate malignity engendered by the late war, and intensified by our late political struggles, will soon be displaced by a broad charity that will enable men to disagree in politics, as in other things, without hating each other; and that our marriage may then take place, not only with the consent, but with the benediction, of your father."

Just at this moment another young man turned a bend in the road, about a hundred yards distant, which brought this conversation abruptly to a close. As the second young man walked leisurely down the road the riders went to meet him at a brisk trot, as if they had only stopped a moment to get a switch with which to urge their horses home more rapidly.

This second young man doffed his hat familiarly to the riders as they passed him in the road. Reaching the glen he turned into the laurel thicket, but was halted at the first step with the command:

" Halt! who comes there ? "

" A ghoul," answered the young man who had just come up, and " a member of Den No. 40."

"Advance with the password," answered the voice in the bushes.

The young man went forward to meet and exchange the secret password of the den with his friend, John Latham.

* * * * * * * *

Before proceeding further with this narrative it is necessary that the persons who have so far appeared should be introduced to the reader.

The young man whom we first found in the laurel bushes was John Latham. He was a handsome fellow, and possessed a magnificent physique. His father had been killed in the war, and his widowed mother, her efforts to rear her son and provide the means of his education, had well-nigh spent all that was left her after the ravages of Sherman's army in his notorious " march to the sea." Young Latham was desperately in love with the young lady whom he heard speak of her plighted faith to her companion of the evening, but from some cause he had deferred mentioning his love to her.

The young man on horseback was Judge Richard Farwell, who had lately come South from the State of Massachusetts. He was at first greeted by the inhabitants of Westville by the opprobrious epithet of " carpetbagger," but by his gentlemanly deportment and manly courage he had, by this time, so far won the confidence and respect of the citizens of the town that very few now applied to him that reproachful title. Indeed, so acceptable to the people had he become that when the resident judge of the judicial district died, he was appointed judge of the district. This was done because no other lawyer in the district could accept the office on account of the " iron-clad oath " which the Federal statute required to be administered to all persons inducted into office. This oath required all officers to swear that they had never given aid or encouragement to the enemies of the United States government, nor accepted office under any government hostile to the United States; and very few persons in the South could take it. Judge Farwell was a man of conspicuous ability and broad culture, but his legal knowledge was quite limited, he having obtained license to practice law only a few weeks before his appointment as judge, under a statute then in force, which allowed any person to become an attorney by simply paying a tax fee of twenty dollars. He had never attended a law school or prepared himself in any way for the duties of his chosen profession; but he possessed an astute and logical mind, and by close application to the study of the law during leisure hours, he so far mastered the rudiments of his profession as to sustain himself with tolerable credit on the bench, though he sometimes made ludicrous mistakes, as might be expected. He was tall and handsome, and as gallant and courageous as any Southern cavalier.

The young lady was Miss Minnie Wyland, and no fairer flower of womanhood ever grew on Southern soil. She would be called a blonde, had blue eyes, rosy cheeks, pearly teeth and was tall and graceful.

She was the daughter of Major James Wyland, who fought on the side of the Confederacy throughout the four long years of the war, and who came out of the war and still remained, an "unreconstructed rebel." He was very tenacious of his own opinions, and intolerant of the opinions of others, and hated capet-baggers and scallawags worse than a Christian hates the devil. He was a lawyer, and so fond of controversy that if you happened to agree with him, even in common conversation, he would immediately take an opposite view of the subject, simply for the sake of argument.

The other young man, who announced himself as a "ghoul of Den No. 40," was Albert Seaton. He was a young man of noble family, polished education, chivalrous disposition, and was as generous and unselfish as any man that ever lived. He had joined the Ku-Klux from a sense of duty.

The reader, no doubt, has already surmised that the meeting of Albert Seaton and John Latham was not by mere accident, and this conjecture is entirely correct.

Almost immediately after the exchange of the password of the den between Latham and Seaton, other

members of the Klan began to assemble at the foot of
the glen, and each one, as he approached and entered
the laurel thicket, was halted and required to give the
password of the evening. These passwords were changed
at every meeting of the Klan, in order to exclude from
participation in the proceedings of their meetings any
person who was not at the time actually co-operating
with the Klan.

The place selected for the meetings of the Klan
seemed to have been specially prepared by the hand of
nature for such a purpose. Glen Echo, in fact, appeared to be nothing less than a great natural amphi-
theatre lying between two mountains, with only one
possible way of entrance or exit. For some distance
from the mouth of the glen the passage between the
cliffs was narrow and difficult, and through this the
ghouls marched in single file until they reached the
broader surface, some distance back, where their secret
meetings were held.

Albert Seaton was Cyclop, or master, of the den. A
local den had no other officers.

As it was one of the rules of the Klan that no word
should be spoken after entering the glen, or cave, except on matters pertaining to business, the Klan proceeded at once to the discharge of the business before it.

"I will hear a report from the committee to investigate the conduct of Peter Tinklepaugh," said the Cyclop, adjusting his cap, which was over two feet high
and on which was painted a rattlesnake, coiled and
ready to spring.

Peter Tinklepaugh was a genuine carpet-bagger from the State of Connecticut. He had been tempted to come South by the same philanthropic motive that prompted so many others to come from that home of virtue, viz., a willingness to take charge of some lucrative office in the gift of the newly-enfranchised negro; but poor Peter had been disappointed as an office-seeker, and had found congenial employment as a school-teacher for the colored children in the vicinity of Kenneth Grove. It was reported of Tinklepaugh that he not only taught the negroes social equality with the whites, but that he had actually set them an example, that fixed at once his status in the social circle, by taking unto himself a wife from among the sable daughters of Ham. It was this charge that the committee had been appointed to investigate. The committee, however, owing to the distance to Kenneth Grove had not completed their investigations, so the matter was continued until next meeting.

"Any charges to be preferred against any one?" again demanded the Cyclop.

Here Sam Washburn handed up the following:

"Richard Farwell, judge. Charges—

"1. Appointing a negro as an officer of court, to-wit: the appointment of Dick Madison as court crier.

"2. Causing negroes to be empanelled as jurors.

"3. Refusing to allow challenges to jurors on account of color."

Sam Washburn was an active and influential member of the Klan, and had the honor of being one of the ten genii of the empire.

Although the charge against judge Farwell was made by Sam Washburn, it will not require any supernatural power of discernment to reach the conclusion that the real author was a young man whose heart was wrung with jealousy, and who had that very evening sworn vengeance against his rival. It was a rule of the Klan that all charges against any person should be presented in writing in a disguised hand, and that a paper containing a charge should never be presented by the person complaining, so that the majority should never know who the real complainant was.

A committee consisting of Sam Washburn, John Latham and Henry Worthel was appointed by the Cyclop to investigate the charge made against judge Farwell, and the committee instructed to report at next meeting.

CHAPTER II.

ANOTHER CARPET-BAGGER INVITED.

When Judge Farwell separated from Minnie Wyland, on reaching home after the eventful ride mentioned in the last chapter, he was in such a state of ecstatic bliss that he actually imagined himself in love with everything that surrounded him. The town of Westville never before seemed half so lovely, nor its broad streets, lined on each side with stately elms, half so enchanting. In the exuberance of his joy, he forgot and forgave the animosities engendered by recent political struggles, while the soft, sweet words of Minnie Wyland drowned even the voice of unjust criticism, which had lately cried out against him with such partisan bitterness.

It was in this state of mind that the judge entered his room at the Midland Hotel, where he found an old servant, Ben Wyland, a former slave of Major James Wyland, just kindling a fire, for though it was in the month of May, and the flowers were in bloom, a little fire after nightfall was not uncomfortable.

"Hello, Uncle Ben," said the judge, "it seems you are a little late in preparing my fire this evening."

"Well, jedge," said Uncle Ben, "I knowed yo' wus gone out ridin' wid Miss Minnie agin, an' I didn't 'spect yo' home till night driv yo' in, so I thought I'd have the fire jes' started like when yo' got here."

"Very well, Uncle Ben," answered the judge, "I have no complaint to make of your tardiness; but how

came you to know I had gone out riding with Miss
Minnie, and what induced you to believe that I would
remain out beyond my usual hour?"

"Never mind," answered Uncle Ben, "I'se gittin' old,
now, and I'se waited on too many young men in love
not to be able to jedge by de praprations an' oder ebi-
dences whar dey gwine when I see 'em start out in de
direcshun ob her house, an' as fur stayin' out late, why,
ob co'se any man would stay out wid sich a gal as Miss
Minnie as long as he could."

"Then you are well acquainted with her, are you,
Uncle Ben?"

"Laws' sake, jedge, ob co'se I is, when I wurked
dar all my life till dis year. I'se knowed her eber
sense she wus a baby, an' a nice gal she is, too."

"I presume you will not find any one to disagree
with you in your estimation of her—at least not here,"
answered the judge. "But did you really belong to
Major Wyland in slavery time, Uncle Ben?"

"Yes, sah, jedge, an' a mighty good massa he wus,
too, do' dey do say he's mighty 'posed to de cullud
man bein' erlowed to vote wid de white folks now.
Dey say he berlongs to de chuck-a-lucks."

"Ku-Klux, I guess you mean, Uncle Ben."

"Yes, sar, I means de chuck-a-lucks what whips de
cullud folks fer votin' an' jining de leags. Dey whipped Uncle Mose Patterson jes befor' las' 'lection an'
skeered him so he dun lef' de country befo' de 'lection
come on."

"Yes, I have heard of the numerous lawless outrages
committed by these bands of assassins in this country,"

answered the judge. "But why have they never mo-
lested you, Uncle Ben? Do you not exercise your
blood-bought privileges as a citizen enough to cast a
vote for the party that gave you your freedom?"

"No, sah. I neber votes now, jedge. I voted once,
an' voted de 'Publicin ticket, but ole massa say it dun
me no good; dat de 'Publicin party dun fooled me
erbout de forty acres an' de mule, an' I tole him I'd
quit votin' till I got de promise."

"You mean by the promise, the forty acres and the
mule, uncle Ben?"

"Yes, sah, dat's it. De 'Publicin party told de cullud men to vote de 'Publicin ticket an' ebery one would
git forty acres ob land an' a mule, an' ole massa tells
me dat foolin' me once wus ernough."

"Very well," answered the judge, a little vexed at
finding any colored man who failed to follow the behests of the Republican party, "we will discuss these
matters some other time, and I think I can show you
it is still your duty to help perpetuate the power of the
party that broke the shackles of slavery from your
ankles. I wish to write a letter now, so you will please
bring my writing materials from the table in the corner
of the room there, and place them on the table before
the fire."

Uncle Ben obeyed this command with the alacrity of
an old-time servant, and having placed the writing
materials on the table, as requested, he bowed respect-
fully to the judge, as he closed the door behind him,
and then picked up his hat, which he had deposited on
the floor just outside the door of the room in the true

style of an *ante bellum* servant, and wended his way to the kitchen.

As soon as he had gone, judge Farwell seized his pen and wrote the following letter to Donald Weston, his old school-mate and friend back in Massachusetts:

"My Dear Weston: You will remember that when I bid you good-bye to come South, I promised you if the Ku-Klux did not hang me as an example to all other carpet-baggers 'in like cases offending,' I would write you my impressions of the country, and would also advise you whether you could afford to risk your own precious carcass among the people of the 'Invisible Empire.' I am happy to inform you that in most respects my highest expectations have been fully realized, and though I am often pained at the recital of tales of vindictive lawlessness on the part of the numerous Ku-Klux-Klans in the country, I find that a vast majority of the people are as law-abiding and as cultured, intelligent and industrious as the people of Massachusetts. I say my highest expectations have been realized; indeed, they have been exceeded. I have been appointed judge of the Superior Courts of this judicial district, and when you come down here (and you must come) you will have to address me as 'Judge Farwell', instead of by the old school-boy name of 'Dick.' It happened in this way: You will remember that the United States Congress passed a law requiring all officers to take and subscribe to an oath to the effect that they had never given aid or encouragement to the enemies of the United States, or held office under any government hostile to the United States. Well, I had just obtained license to practice law in this State, under a State statute authorizing any person to practice law who would pay a tax fee of twenty dollars, when the judge of this judicial district died, and it so happened that no other lawyer in the district could take the oath of office required by the act of Congress, and so I received the appointment of judge without ever having read Blackstone or Kent. This district is filled with lawyers of eminent ability, some of them are really brilliant, but all of them are very kind to me, and treat me with the greatest courtesy.

"Now, what I wish to impress upon your mind most particularly in this letter, is that you may strike the same good fortune by coming to this county and coming *at once.* The State solicitor (prosecuting attorney) of this judicial district is very old and feeble, and he promises to resign in favor of any young man who will accept the position and who belongs to the Republican party, and by coming at once you can get the position. No native young man can take the place because all who have the requisite education belong to the opposing party. All you have to do is to come before me at the beginning of next term of the Superior Court, with a certificate of good moral character and the clerk's receipt for the tax fee of twenty dollars, and I will grant your license. Bring your certificate of good moral character with you, *and come at once.*

"Now, a few words as to the social and political conditions of this country : Although several years have elapsed since the cessation at Appomatox of actual hos-

tilities, the political sea is by no means serene; but the
surges of the great commotion still continue to agitate
the waters, notwithstanding the tempest has subsided.
The political caldron boils with fury, and the fuel that
feeds the flames is composed of the animosities of the
old slavery contest. Numerous secret political societies exist, and the political intrigues are concocted with
satanic ingenuity, and are executed, when necessary,
by the hands of assassins, and this, too, with impunity.
The most formidable of these secret political organizations is, as you have no doubt already learned, the
Ku-Klux-Klan, a secret, oath-bound organization, whose
chief object is the suppression of the negro as a fac-
tor in politics. These 'Klans' are well organized, and
fully equipped for any devilment that may be suggested. Their local lodges are usually denominated
dens, while the members of these dens or Klans are
called *gouls*, and the presiding officers, or masters, are
called *Cyclops*. A county is a *province*, and is governed
by a *grand giant* and four *goblins*. A congressional
district is a *dominion*, governed by a grand *Titan* and
six furies; a State is a *realm*, governed by a grand dragon
and eight hydras, and the whole country is an empire,
governed by a grand *wizard* and ten *genii*. Their ban-
ner is triangular, on which is painted a black dragon on
a yellow field with a red border. Their dress consists
of a long, loose gown of any color selected by each
particular Klan, and a covering for the head descending
to the breast. This head-dress is usually decorated in
some startling and fantastic manner, and the wearer is
an object of terror to all beholders, especially to the

superstitious colored man. The top of this head-dress is cone-shaped, being supported by small wires, and often reaches two feet above the head of the wearer.

"The numerous murders, whippings, burnings and other depredations committed by these marauding bands, have created a reign of terror in this country, but I have instructed the grand juries in all the counties in my judicial district to investigate these matters, and to return indictments against all offenders, and I am hopeful that a few convictions of some of the leading spirits, followed by a condign punishment, will restore peace and harmony, and insure the public safety.

"Now, my dear Weston, I have presented the darkest side of the picture to you, simply because I have written mainly of the political situation here; but I have a brighter side of the picture to show you when I see you, and I assure you in conclusion that when you come you will find much to love and admire in these Southern people, notwithstanding their bitter partisan prejudices, social caste and sectional hatred. This country is now taking on a new life, and there are many opportunities here for political preferment and honor, and for the accumulation of wealth. You will be called a 'carpet-bagger,' of course, but do not let that reproachful epithet deter you from coming. The ultra-partisans of the Bourbon Democracy call all persons from the North, who come to make their homes in the South, 'carpet-baggers;' but the term is more generally applied to those who become seekers of the office, while all native white persons who affiliate with the Republican party

2

are called 'scallawags.' Against this latter class vindictive prejudice vents its direst spleen, and Democratic orators exhaust their powers of invective. They are excommunicated from the church, ostracised from society, and whipped and scourged by the Ku-Klux. Nevertheless, you will find a number of intelligent white men who are still loyal to the cause of the Union, and who can take the 'test oath' without any scruples of conscience.

"Trusting that I may be favored with a speedy reply, or, what is better still, that you will answer in person, I remain,

"Very truly your friend,

"RICHARD FARWELL."

Whoever heard of a young man just entering upon the threshold of manhood refusing to accept a respectable and lucrative office? Certainly no such charge was ever preferred against the reputation of any one of the horde of carpet-baggers who invaded the South just after the late war, as the Goths and Huns once invaded Europe, and who corrupted and debauched the public morals, bankrupted our governments, and destroyed public credit. And so it was with our new acquaintance, Donald Weston, as the following letter in answer to the above will show:

"MY DEAR JUDGE:—You see I recognize the dignity of your new position at once by discarding the old familiar name of "Dick," and addressing you by the title of your office. You cannot imagine how surprised

I was when I read that you had obtained license to
practice law without the usual requisite preparation,
and that you had been appointed judge without ever
having had a client; but my astonishment reached its
climax when I read further on that almost a similar
position was within my own grasp and on similar terms.
Of course I will come, and of course I will accept the
office tendered ; and when once I am installed in office,
all I want is a volume of precedents from which to
draw indictments against the members of those infa-
mous Ku-Klux Klans for their lawless depredations,
Trust me to be with you as soon as I can make the
necessary arrangements for my departure from home.

"Mother and my two sisters send their kindest personal regards.

   " Yours,   " DONALD WESTON."

CHAPTER III.

A DISCOVERY.

In the first chapter it was stated that Albert Seaton had joined the Ku-Klux from a sense of duty, but the reader was not informed how that sense of duty arose and how it impelled him to become a member of the Klan.

Let us take a cursory glance at his history and a brief survey of his surroundings, at the period covered by this story, and we shall see.

He was born in 1847, and consequently was just a little too young to be conscripted into the service of the Confederate army before the surrender at Appomattox; but he was old enough to remember and appreciate Sherman's famous "march to the sea," and the raids and depredations of the victorious Northern army on its homeward march after the close of the great conflict.

In 1870 he still lived with his mother and sister at Cherrycroft, the old Seaton homestead; but every glance at the premises, in their dilapidated condition, recalled the devastation committed by Sherman's victorious army when that famous Federal commander descended upon the eastern portion of Georgia and the Carolinas, and with the hand of Hyder Ali made desolate the fairest country on earth, burned all the barns and gin-houses, pillaged the stores, confiscated all the horses and mules, scared all the women and children into hysterical fits, and left them destitute of the simplest means of subsistence. Well he remembered the night when Gen. Sherman took quarters for himself and staff in Cherrycroft. He had stood, with his trembling mother and little sister, on the broad piazza in the presence of the dreaded General, and had heard the command given to apply the torch to every building on the premises, save the dwelling in which they were quartered. And well he remembered, too, that while the flames from more than a dozen barns and gin-houses in the community were observed soaring higher toward heaven than the spirits of some of those who applied the torches will ever reach, the same famous General taunted them with the remark: "It does me good to see these flames lighting up the elements at night; it shows that my men are at work."*

This was young Seaton's first introduction to the Republican party.

But there was another scene that made a more indelible impression on the mind of the young man, and that had a more potent influence in shaping the course and destiny of his life. His father, Col. Albert Seaton, Sr., fought throughout the four weary years of the war, and surrendered only with his beloved commander under the famous apple-tree. With a heart heavy with disappointment, humiliated and discouraged, ragged, dirty, bleeding and hungry, he turned his face once more toward home. Visions of that beautiful home, surrounded by a magnificent grove and substantial out-houses, flitted across his mind, as step by step, he

*Historical.

wended his way thitherward with bleeding feet. In
his imagination, he saw his beautiful wife and the two
children, coming down the lane to meet him and greet
him with kisses of affection. IIis wife and children
did meet him and greet him with kisses and tears of
joy, but the roses of beauty had faded from the cheeks
of his wife; her eyes, like her cheeks, were sunken and
hollow, and her voice, so long accustomed to utter the
plaints of misfortune and disappointment, was tremulous and weak, while his children, the descendants of a
noble and once opulent family, were actually famish-
ing for bread.

Col. Seaton reached home a few weeks in advance of
the advent in his vicinity of the victorious Federal soldiery, who, on their homeward march, pillaged, plundered, confiscated, squandered and stole everything
that the iron-heel of war had not destroyed. With that
indomitable courage and energy so characteristic of the
Southern hero, he set about at once to repair his wasted
fortunes. He had just finished planting a belated crop,
himself and son both taking a hand at the plow, when
another Federal officer with his command reached the
neighborhood and camped for the night on the plantation. Soon after nightfall a band of stragglers set out
for a raid in the neighborhood, but soon returned with
the news that they had found the dead body of a Northern soldier in the fence-corner down at the foot of the
lane leading up to the house of Col. Seaton. Death to
these men was a familiar thing, but the sight of a dead
body on the field of battle was quite a different thing
from the sight of a dead soldier by the road-side after

the cessation of hostilities, and demand was made for
an investigation as to the cause of death. The skull
of the dead man was crushed in, as if by a blow inflicted
with some dull, heavy instrument, and there could be
no doubt of the fact that the poor fellow had met his
death by violence.

Accordingly, a court-martial was ordered, and all the
negroes of the neighborhood were subpœnaed as witnesses. A few whites were also examined, but it was
thought unnecessary to subpœna those who would not
voluntarily appear and testify, and all who failed to
so appear were forthwith accused of the murder. After
a most patient investigation, no clue as to who the murderer was could be discovered (the negro who killed
the Yankee with a pine knot in a quarrel over a bottle
of liquor having testified that he knew nothing about
it), but the blood of a Northern soldier had been spilled,
and his surviving brethren, whose thirst for the blood
of the men in tattered gray had not been satiated during the war, now clamored for the life of some Southern man in expiation of the crime.

Then it was that the Federal commander adopted a
novel plan for avenging the death of the dead com-
rade, a plan hitherto unknown in the annals of war, and
for which Grotius gives us no precedent. It was ordered
that slips of white paper, representing in number all the
white men in the coummmunity for five miles around,
should be placed in a hat; that a cross mark should be
made on one of the slips, and that, after shuffling them
carefully, each man in the community within the prescribed limits should draw a paper from the hat, and that

the man who drew the paper having the cross mark on it should be immediately condemned to be shot.

Col. Seaton took his position in the line that marched toward the fated hat, with an uneasy presentiment that he was to be the victim. His wife and children stood a few steps to one side, but not so far off but that he could see the palid countenance and trembling lips of his dear wife, as she watched, with bated breath, each man as he placed his hand in the hat and drew forth a blank paper, every blank drawn lessening the chances of escape for her husband. At last Col. Seaton's turn came; he placed his hand in the hat and drew forth a paper, and his presentiment was verified. With one wild leap he cleared the line of Federal soldiery, and the next moment he was bounding through the woods on a race for life. The order to follow and capture him was quickly given, and a score of blue coats, some mounted and some afoot, joined in the pursuit. The moon was shining brightly, and the flying form of the condemned man could be plainly seen as he crossed a small clearing before reaching the heavy woods. A volley of shot followed him, and as the report of the guns died on the night air, Mrs. Seaton swooned, and was conveyed by her terrified son into the house. She wrote to the Federal commander after he had gone, asking to be informed of the fate of her husband, at at least to know his burial place, but he deigned her no reply.

And such was young Albert's second introduction to the Republican party.

Nor had his experience with that party inspired him

with confidence in its teachings and principles, or respect for its votaries. The first time he ever attempted
to exercise his right to vote after attaining his majority, he found a miserable, one-eyed carpet-bagger from
Maine, and two negroes, sitting as judges of election,
and a motley crew, composed of carpet-baggers, scalawags, and negroes around the polls. A large number of the intelligent and respectable portion of the
community, he was informed, were not permitted to
vote, over thirty thousand in the State being deprived
of their elective franchise under the "iron-clad oath,"
required by the act of Congress of February 20, 1867,
which gave the colored men the ballot, but disfran-
chised, in many instances, their late masters. The
ballot-boxes, at the close of the day, were taken in charge
by the one-eyed carpet-bagger from Maine, who afterwards transmitted them to the Military Governor appointed by President Johnson to take charge of the
Provincial State government, who counted the ballots
and certified the returns, according to his own sweet
will, to the authorities at the State capital. This and
and other disgraceful scenes caused young Seaton to
look with the apprehension of a statesman upon the
continued encroachments of the dominant party upon
what was left of Southern autonomy. He saw around
him thousands of illiterate and inexperienced colored
voters, led by unprincipled and designing adventurers,
who concocted and carried into effect the most flagrant
and disgusting schemes of pecuniary plunder that ever
human ingenuity invented, or venal avarice carried
into execution. He knew also that these colored voters

had been organized into a great secret society, the object of which was to perpetuate the reign of the Republican party, and that they had been instructed and taught to believe that their late masters were their inveterate enemies; that the white man only waited for the power to place the manacles of slavery around their feet again, and that it was proper and right that they should "spoil the Egyptians" by pillaging, plundering, burning and murdering, if necessary, to enhance the interests of the party. In such a state of affairs it was but natural that a young, hot-blooded youth, stung to desperation by the remembrance of the indignities heaped upon his father's family, the wanton destruction of their property, and of the inhuman murder of his father, should join the Ku-Klux, the object of which was to counteract the measures of the Union League and protect society.

    *   *   *   *   *   *   *

Begging pardon for the digression which was necessary, in order to explain Albert Seaton's connection with the Klan, I will now conduct the reader again to Glen Cove, but this time by a more circuitous route.

The forenoon of the day appointed for the next meeting of the Klan was rainy and gloomy, and John Latham sat in his room and looked out upon the muddy streets of Westville, with an uneasy foreboding that the rain might interfere and prevent the meeting; but about noon the clouds broke and drifted away, the sun shone out, and everything gave promise of a serene and beautiful evening. It was a splendid day for squirrel hunting, and there were plenty of them in the high hills around Glen Echo, and the idea occurred to John that he would get Sam Washburn and Henry Worthel, and they would repair to the hills to spend the afternoon in that delightful sport and recreation. Of course, no one will be so uncharitable as to charge that a young man, who simply takes his gun and calls his dog to go hunting, in company with a couple of friends, could have any sinister motive in view, or wicked purpose to serve, and, therefore, no importance should be attached to the fact that just before starting out to find his two friends he placed a small bundle of papers in his shot-pouch, and gave a malicious chuckle. Henry Worthel was clerk at the Midland Hotel where Judge Farwell boarded, but the judge was then at the court-house, hearing an important application for a writ of *habeas corpus*, filed by a man who had been imprisoned on a charge of killing a negro preacher, and so our friend, Latham, did not have to encounter the glance of his successful rival on going to the hotel. He found Henry Worthel at his desk in the hotel office, ready to accept the cash at the rate of two dollars per day from every departing guest, in exchange for the meagre fare served by uncle Ben and a dusky maiden by the name of Millie.

"Look here, Henry," said John as he sauntered into the hotel office with an air that might have indicated to a stranger that he was the proprietor of the place, "how would you like to beg off this afternoon and go squirrel hunting on the hills around Glen Echo? The rain this morning and the succeeding sunshine have made it a most auspicious time for such sport."

"I quite agree with you," answered Henry, "that it is a splendid time for that purpose, but will we not vio-

late one of the rules of the Klan by allowing ourselves
to be seen lurking in the neighborhood of the glen before night?"

"O, pshaw!" answered John, looking carefully around
to see that no one overheard this conversation; "what
member of the Klan would be idiotic enough to accuse
us of lurking in the vicinity of the den when we hunt
with guns and dogs and make noise enough to wake
the dead? It may be that we shall find some member
of the Union League lurking around, though, and if so,
we can take him off instead of a squirrel, and so serve
the country better."

"No, we will not be likely to find any of them out
this evening," said Henry. "They had their meeting
last night at the Cross Roads school-house, so Sam
Washburn informs me, and as their meeting lasted
nearly all night, I think very few of them have energy
enough to stir out much to-day."

"An all-night meeting would indicate the transaction
of important business," said John, "and we must ascertain what it was. I presume that carpet-bagger judge
was there, directing them in their devilty."

"I do not know who were present, or what they
did," said Henry. "You know our spy never discloses
professional secrets, except in open meeting of the
Klan."

"And that reminds me of the fact that he is to make
one of our hunting party," answered John; "so get
ready and we will be off, and will stop in after him."

The person here designated as "the spy" was Samuel Washburn, who has been partially introduced to
the reader already. It may seem strange to speak of

the existence of professional spies so many years after
the beligerent armies had been disbanded, but the private citizen may learn many useful lessons from the
manœuvres of an army, and many military tactics may be adopted and used to advantage by the
civilians. The Ku-Klux Klan was organized for the
purpose of countervailing the wicked measures of the
Union League, and as the League in the vicinity of
Westville had resolved upon a regular system of depredations, by burning and otherwise destroying the
property of the white respectable people of the community, it became necessary, in order to circumvent
such wicked designs, to ascertain every proposed movement of the enemy in advance, and hence " Klan No.
40 " had resorted to the military expedient of employ-
ing spies, who were required to work their way into
the League, and to report all plans and intended movements to the Klan. Through this system of espionage
the Klan was enabled to avert many direful calamities,
threatened to be visited by the League upon the people of the community in retaliation for outrages alleged
to have been committed by the Ku-Klux.

Sam Washburn was a "hail fellow well met " to
everybody, and this description of him, so far as his
manners are concerned, is sufficient. He was, withal,
a sharp, shrewd politician, as ingenious as the devil
in forming his designs, and as bold as a lion in executing them, and his service as a spy for the Ku-Klux
gave him an opportinity of displaying his subtelty and
bravery in a way that secured for him the admiration,
as well as the confidence, of every member of the
Klan.

He was soon found, and as his jolly disposition made
him an enthusiastic sportsman, as well as a successful
spy, he readily joined the hunting expedition, but insisted that they should go by Cherrycroft for Albert
Seaton.

To this proposition Henry Worthel readily assented,
but John Latham did so rather reluctantly, and placed
his hand on the bundle of papers in his shot-pouch with
an expression of uneasiness in his countenance, as much
as to say that he preferred to have along none but the
original hunting party—in short, none but the members
of the committee appointed to investigate the charges
preferred at the last meeting of the Klan against Judge
Farwell; for the truth is, that John had planned this
hunting expedition for the sole purpose of having the
committee consider the charges and formulate their
report, and the bundle of papers referred to was simply
copies from the record of the Superior Court of West
County, giving evidence to sustain the charge preferred
at the last meeting of the Klan. He knew that Sam felt
rather kindly disposed toward the judge, on account of
some recent favors, and so wished for more time than
they would have on the road between town and Cherrycroft, within which to poison Sam's mind against the
judge and induce him to recommend rigorous punishment; but seeing his plans frustrated, in part, he resolved
to make the best of his opportunity, and if he could not
induce Sam to recommend the punishment which, in
his opinion, the magnitude of the offense deserved, he
would try and have the report submitted without
recommendation as to the punishment to be inflicted,

leaving that to be determined by the ghouls of the Klan. The judge's real offense, so far as John Latham was concerned, was his presumption in falling in love with Minnie Wyland, but such presumptuousness, in John's estimation, was a crime which deserved the severest penalty.

"Well, boys," said John, as soon as they had left behind them the last suburban residence and had passed the line of incorporation marked with the words "Town Boundary", on a stone planted by the roadside, "I presume that you have not forgotten your appointment on the committee to investigate the conduct of the imported carpet-bagger judge."

"No," answered Henry Worthel, "I have not entirely forgotten the fact of my appointment on the committee, but I am afraid I shall have to call into requisition the ingenuity of our worthy spy to invent for me some excuse for my remissness in failing to make a proper investigation, unless his power of invention shall be exhausted in framing an excuse for himself."

"Oh, no," said Sam, "I never bother myself with excuses."

"Nor I, either," answered John Latham, "and in this particular instance I am under no necessity of doing so, for I have in my possession certified copies of the records of our Superior Court, which will fully sustain the charge made against him by our Klan."

It will be noticed that John spoke of the charges as having been made by "our Klan," for he was careful to avoid all suspicion of his personal interest in the matter, and not even Sam Washburn, who presented the written charges, knew who the real author was.

"As for my part," said Henry Worthel, "I have become so thoroughly disgusted with his social equality
ideas, as exhibited about the hotel where he boards, that
I am willing to sign a report sustaining the charges on
a simple inspection of the copies of the records. I am
tired of hearing a negro wench addressed as "Miss,"
and of seeing the servants all treated as the social
equals of the proprietor and guests of the hotel."

"Well," said Sam, "let us see your certified copies
of the record, John, and we will sit down here on this
log and make out whatever report we can agree upon."

They all three sat down on the log pointed out by
Sam, and John Latham proceeded to unroll his certified copies of the records, with as much seriousness and
dignity as is usually displayed by a negro preacher on
opening the Bible for the purpose of taking his text.

The first case appearing on the records showed that
judge Farwell had sustained a challenge to a juror on
the ground that the defendant on trial was a colored
man, and that the juror had expressed the opinion that
he could not do impartial justice between the State and
a colored person on trial, charged with burning the barn
of a white person. This challenge was made by an
insolent little twenty-dollar lawyer, and the judge sustained it on the ground that antipathy between the
races was evidence of sufficient personal ill-will to dis-
qualify the juror.

The next case was one in which the prosecuting attorney for the State was permitted by the Court to
ask each juror on the original panel if he had any feeling or prejudice which would prevent the juror from

returning a verdict of guilty against a white man for killing a negro. In this case the solicitor for the State was also permitted by the Court to ask each juror if he did not belong to a secret organization which had imposed upon him an oath or obligation, beside which an oath administered in a Court of Justice, if in conflict with the oath imposed by such secret order, would be disregarded. This last challenge was considered as a direct thrust at the Ku-Klux, and as an unwarranted interference on the part of the Court with the consciences of its members.

In the next case the charge was that the judge, after the grand jury had returned a bill in open court with the endorsement "not a true bill," had refused to receive this return; but had ordered the grand jury to be brought into court and placed in the box occupied by the trial jury, and that he had there publicly examined them himself, and had instructed the grand jury that if they believed the evidence they should reverse their former decision and return the bill endorsed "a true bill." This was considered an unwarranted interference with the province of the grand jury, and a dangerous and revolutionary subversion of that ancient system of a secret investigation as to the commission of crime. In this case it appeared, by certificate of the Supreme Court, that even a Republican Supreme Court had reversed the decision of the court below, and had held that the action of the judge of the Superior Court in thus examining the witnesses before the grand jury in public was a dangerous departure from the ordinary course of procedure in our courts of justice.

Although several similar cases were shown by the

3

record, only one other was considered by the committee, as those enumerated were declared to be sufficient to sustain the charge. The other case considered, was one in which judge Farwell had directed the sheriff to summon from among the bystanders colored jurors in a civil suit between a white man and a negro.

These records were adjudged sufficient to sustain the allegations contained in the written charge, presented against judge Farwell at the last meeting of the Klan, and a report in accordance therewith was unanimously agreed upon and signed by the committee.

After the signing of the report the committee, or rather, the hunting party now, since their duties as a committee had been discharged for the time, were joined by Albert Seaton, whom they found on the roadside before reaching the house, and the four proceeded at once to the hills around Glen Echo.

Just before reaching the foot of the narrow gorge where the road crosses it, they were startled by a low, rumbling noise, somewhat resembling the sound of an earthquake, which seemed to be rapidly approaching, and which immediately threw them into a state of the wildest consternation. They gazed at each other for a moment in mute bewilderment, and on their countenances were depicted evidences of the wildest despair. The bravest among them (the spy) spoke first.

"A cyclone boys, let us fly to the rocks at the head of Glen Echo for shelter!"

The words were scarcely uttered before the spy was dashing up the narrow gorge, with the rapidity of an excited fawn, with the others close at his heels. The winds were howling and groaning as they swept around the tops of the hills, and the tall oaks and poplars were swaying to and fro like reeds, when the four reached a cave in the side of the hill at the upper extremity of the glen and darted in, like rabbits pursued by hounds. They had barely become ensconced in the cave when a huge rock, or boulder, became disengaged from its fastenings near the top of the hill by the uprooting of a tree, and came tumbling down, passing over the mouth of the cave in which the hunters had taken refuge.

"By George," said Sam, "it begins to look a little like the day·of judgment had come, when the wicked are to cry out for the rocks and hills to fall on them and for the mountains to cover them, but as I am not yet ready to begin the cry, I am going to penetrate a little further and see whether the elements of the infernal regions have all been turned loose on top of the earth."

"What is that?" said Albert Seaton as, in attempting to follow Sam, he stepped on something, which rolled from under his feet and threw him to the ground. "I stepped on something which I am sure was not a stone."

"Here it is," said John, who was immediately behind Albert, "and it is a bottle. What a queer place for a bottle. And there is something in it, too," he said, as he picked it up and held it in a little streak of light that penetrated through a crevice between two large rocks near the mouth of the cave. "I believe it is a paper though," he jocularly remarked, "instead of whiskey."

"Look here, boys," said Sam, turning round to face the others while his countenance, even in the dim light, showed signs of intense excitement, "things are getting serious in here as well as on the outside. Do you see those bones there? Somebody has died in here, and this is his tomb we are in."

Each gazed at the others with an expression of utter bewilderment Before them lay the bones of the unknown dead, while outside the cave a most terrific storm raged and howled.

At last it was suggested that they examine the paper in the bottle, and coming back as near the mouth of the cave as prudence and safety would permit, Albert Seaton took the bottle and broke it over a stone, and began to read from the paper. With the first sentence he faltered and failed, and dropping the paper on the ground, he buried his face in his hands in a paroxysm of excitement and grief. The very first few words had revealed to him the terrible truth that the bones that lay before him were his father's skeleton?

There were two papers in the bottle, and the one from which Albert had commenced to read was as follows:

"My DEAR WIFE: I have been shot by the Yankees, and am bleeding to death in this cave, in which I have taken refuge from their brutal attacks.

"I have with me a note signed by the board of county commissioners of West County, and I deposit it with this letter in a bottle which I happen to have in my pocket, having carried a sick laborer a drink of brandy in it to-day. The note is for six thousand dollars, and was given for salt furnished the poor people of the

county by me during the war at the request of the
county authorities. I want you to collect it as soon as
our county becomes able to pay it, and use the money
in defraying the expenses of completing the education
of our two dear children. Alas, I shall never see the
dear children nor you again, and it may be that you
will never even hear how I died, but I trust to a kind
Providence to direct the step of some kind person to
this cave. I am dying, I know, and my strength is
gone, and I lay down my pencil with a prayer for all.
God bless you all.

   " Your loving husband,

      "ALBERT SEATON, SR."

  The storm subsided at last, and Albert returned to
break the news to his mother and sister. His three
companions hastened back to town with the report of
the wonderful discovery, and afterwards assisted other
kind hands in preparing for the fleshless remains of
the lamented dead a more befitting tomb.

CHAPER IV.

HOW A KU-KLUX MANDATE WAS EXECUTED.

Mrs. Seaton possessed a nervous, excitable temperament, and had been in feeble health for a year or more, and the shock to her nervous system, occasioned by the startling discovery of the skeleton remains of her late husband, threw her in bed, completely prostrated and helpless. Albert immediately despatched a messenger for their family physician, Dr. Taylor Wyland, who was a brother of Major James Wyland, and the doctor assured them that there was no positive danger, but still Albert remained with his mother almost night and day, and was so assiduous in his attentions to her that it was several days before he saw any of the members of the Klan or learned anything about the proceedings of the last meeting. At last Mrs. Seaton become so far convalescent as to permit him to leave her for a few hours, and after a brief consultation with his mother and sister in regard to the propriety of instituting proceedings for the collection of the notes found in the bottle in the cave, it was resolved that Albert should place them in the hands of Major Wyland, the leading lawyer of the county, with instructions to enforce their payment. Accordingly Albert set out for Westville with the notes, but was met on the road by Sam Washburn.

"Good morning, Albert," said Sam, in a tone that indicated that he remembered the incident of a few

days before in the cave, and that he fully sympathized
with Albert in his afflictions. "I was just coming out
to see you. Knowing that you had been confined to
the house for several days, and having heard that your
good mother was much better this morning, it occurred to me that it might do you good to take a jaunt
with me across the country on horseback, and see how
the orders of the Klan were enforced."

"A good ride would greatly benefit me, I have no
doubt, Sam," answered Albert, "and I have no doubt,
I would enjoy witnessing the execution of a Ku-Klux
mandate, provided I could be thoroughly convinced
that the sentence was just and there was no blood in
it; but I am sorry to say that a business errand pre-
vents a compliance with your request to-day."

"As for the justness or severity of the sentence," said
Sam, "you need not be alarmed, for I am sure the rigor
of the punishment is by no means in proportion to the
heinousness of the offense. The charge of miscegena-
tion against Peter Tinklepaugh has been sustained by
the proof, and the simple judgment of the Klan is that
he be whipped with thirty-nine lashes and be ducked in
the river, and I am sure you would enjoy the ducking
even if you should think the whipping a little tough."

"I quite agree with you," said Albert, "that inter-
marriage between the races is a sin against society that
demands rigorous and speedy correction. I consider
it an innovation and a serious onslaught upon our manners and society, and the introduction and practice of
such an evil by Northern carpet-baggers simply shows,
the malignity of the Republican party as well as the

deplorable depravity of those who are so heathenish as
to practice such a revolting social sin. It seems that
the Republican party is not satisfied with taking possession of our government and overthrowing our institutions and destroying our credit, but they seek to extend their reconstruction measures even into our social
system, and destroy all social caste."

"Well, as for my part," answered Sam, "I am in
favor of exterminating all who teach the amalgama-
tion of the races, whether carpet-baggers or scalawags,
and as our den has seen fit to impose a lighter sentence
on the negro-loving pedagogue, I have determined to
see that the lash is firmly applied to the back of Tinklepaugh, and that he receives a sound ducking afterwards."

"All right," answered Albert, "go and see that the
sentence is well carried out, and each time the lash is
applied you may proclaim that 'them's my sentiments.'
I am only sorry that I cannot go with you."

"But why can't you go?" asked Sam. "We will be
back before day in the morning, and unless your business is of pressing importance you can attend to it
then."

"My business is simply to place the notes against the
county, found with my father's remains, in the hands
of Major Wyland for collection," said Albert. "My
mother had abandoned the idea of trying to enforce
their payment long ago, thinking that father had given
them up to the county authorities, on his return from
the war, on account of the impoverished condition of
the people at that time; but our county is now well

able to pay them, and after reading father's instructions we have decided to collect the notes."

"I did not mean to be so impertinent as to inquire into the nature of your business," answered Sam, "but I am glad you have determined to collect the notes, and wish you success in your efforts. But there is no use in your going to town to-day. The notes will have to be presented to the board of county commissioners and demand made of them for their payment before suit can be brought, and as the board does not meet until next Monday, you can take them to Maj. Wyland to-morrow or any day this week just as well as to-day, so come on and lets pay our respects to the noble Peter Tinklepaugh."

"All right," said Albert, "I had not thought about the requirement that the notes should be first presented to the county commissioners, and as my business can be as well attended to to-morrow, I will consent to go with you, but I must first return home, and let mother know I will not be back until after night."

It took Albert only a few moments to return home, and acquaint his mother with his intention to leave off his visit to Major Wyland for that day, and soon the two young men were galloping on their way to Kenneth Grove, where they were to meet the members of the Klan of the Wizard Ghouls, who had been appointed by that Klan to execute the sentence against Peter Tinklepaugh, imposed by Klan No. 40.

It was a rule among the Ku-Klux that all sentences imposed by any Klan should be executed by the ghouls of some other Klan, remote from the vicinity in which the trouble complained of originated, and hence the sentence against Peter Tinklepaugh, declared by Klan No. 40, was sent to the Klan of the Wizard Ghouls to be executed. The reason the decrees of one Klan were always carried out by another was to prevent suspicion and detection, as the victim was not so likely to iden- tify strangers as neighbors.

When night closed in Albert and Sam were only a few miles from the appointed rendezvous, and after assuming their disguises, they pushed on at a rapid pace, and soon found themselves confronted with the most frightful looking apparition they had ever encountered. It was the outside sentinel of the Klan of the Wizard Ghouls, and notwithstanding the fact that they were both thoroughly familiar with Ku-Klux disguises, they had never before beheld anything so hideous and fright- ful. The sentinel wore a long white gown, which was profusely decorated with the most fantastic pictures of hobgoblins and spectres, painted in red and black, while his head dress, which descended to his shoulders and had holes for the eyes, nose and mouth, reached at least three feet above his head, and was covered with red and black stripes, except that on the front a skull and cross-bones were painted. The horse, he rode, was also covered with a sheet similarly ornamented, and had his feet muffled in such a manner that his tread was almost noiseless.

Sam and Albert both gave the sign of recognition at ten paces, and then advanced and exchanged the annual pass-word and the grip with the sentinel. They then advanced to where the main body of the Klan were

stationed, ready to receive their orders to move on.
After a few moments spent in muffling the feet of the
horses rode by Sam and Albert, the sentinels were
called in by a low and peculiar whistle from the Cyclop,
and the whole body were ordered to proceed to the
execution of the decree of Klan No. 40. There were
about twenty persons in the crowd, and they were all
thoroughly disguised, because Peter Tinklepaugh was
a shrewd and intelligent scoundrel, and it was considered necessary to adopt every possible precaution to
prevent detection. There was no blast of the trumpet
or deafening drum-beat to herald their approach, but so
silently and noiselessly did they go that their presence
was first announced to poor Tinklepaugh by the appearance of two ghouls in their frightful disguises
standing in the open door of his house.

At sight of the grim spectres the sable wife of the
social reconstructionist fainted with fear, but the ad-
venturous little pedagogue was not so easily disconcerted. He had ventured to assume the position of
teacher in a colored school, fully realizing the odium
that attached to such an occupation, and fully cognizant of the fact that the country was in a turbulent
state, and that race prejudice was the most combusti-
ble fuel that fed the flames of passion at that particular period of our history, and having received several
Ku-Klux warnings, for the Ku-Klux, like a rattlesnake,
never struck a foe without first warning him of the im-
pending danger, and he was not altogether unprepared
for the perilous crisis that he imagined had arrived.
Rising with cool composure from a table at which he

had been writing, he deliberately, and with perfect
self-possession, placed in a drawer in the side of the
table a few sheets of paper on which he had written a
horrifying account of some imaginary Ku-Klux outrages for a Northern newspaper, and on which his
dusky consort had just been gazing with all the astonishment and imbecility of comprehension manifested
by the Indians while observing the wonderful "talking
paper" of Captain John Smith. Then taking a large
revolver from the same drawer in which he had placed
the paper, he demanded to know what the intrusion
meant.

"O, there is no use in your kicking," answered one
of the ghouls as he glanced at the pistol in the hands
of the imperturbable little teacher, "you've been noti-
fied that we wouldn't tolerate your conduct any longer,
and have been advised to leave the community, and
now we have determined that you shall leave it."

"I do not care a fig for the orders and decrees of a
lawless Ku-Klux-Klan," boldly answered the little man,
"and I have determined to pursue whatever avocation
I may fancy, and to choose as a companion the one
whom I find most congenial."

At this moment the door opposite the one first entered fairly flew off its beings and the room was immediately filled with men in disguise. Poor Tinklepaugh
fully believed that his hour had come, but he was determined to die game, and taking deliberate aim at the
person nearest him, he fired; but as Henry Clay said, in
describing a duel fought by him with John Randolph,
who appeared on the field of honor clad in a long,

loose gown, the ball pierced the middle of the object in front, but the thin, swarthy form of the man within was not there.

Before Tinklepaugh could put his finger to the trigger again, the pistol was knocked out of his hand, and he was bound and gagged before he could utter another word. A rope was tied around his neck in true hangman's style, and he was immediately placed on a horse, and the crowd started for the river, it having been hastily decided that they would proceed to duck him first in order to cool off his anger and calm his vicious spirit, and then flog him to warm him up again and produce a reaction.

It was not far to the river, but still the time consumed on the way gave poor Tinklepaugh, who now fully believed he was to be hung, instead of being allowed to be shot while defending his own home, as he at first anticipated, ample opportunity for reflection, and in this short time he saw, as if in a mirror, his whole past life pass before him in review. He looked back across the years gone by, and saw himself, a little child again holding to his mother's knees while his father, an esteemed minister of the gospel, read some favorite and comforting passage of scripture, and then expounded it in his simple, forcible way. A little further on in the picture he saw himself, a young man standing before the hymeneal altar in a Northern village church, with his lovely bride leaning on his arm, and he heard again the old church organ as it pealed forth the glad wedding march, while he received the congratulations of friends. Then he saw the battlefields of the late war, where the courage and valor he displayed won for him the encomiums of Federal commanders high in authority, and where death, if it had only come to him then, would have found him ready to die a soldier's death and offer himself as a sacrifice on the altar of his country. Again he saw his faithful, but discarded, wife in their little cottage home in the Northern village within sight of the church in which they were married, and he heard the innocent prattle of his own little blue-eyed boy, as he clung to his mother's knees, just as he himself had done in the first picture. And, lastly, he remembered how all his hopes of political preferment had been blasted and blighted in their incipiency, and how all his money had been squandered and wasted in unholy speculation, and then he thought of his disgraceful, bigamous marriage with the miserable negro wench he had just left, and so thinking they reached the river.

At the river brink they all halted, and the gags were taken off Tinklepaugh to prevent drowning him. Hitherto his fear had been that they were going to hang him, but now he became convinced that he was to be drowned. Certainly it was intended to tie a stone to the rope and throw him in the river.

At sight of the rolling waters of the river all his courage deserted him, and the thought of being thrown into the river, with a stone fastened to his neck, transformed him into a cringing, fawning coward. But in all his perplexities his wit and cunning never deserted him, and in order to escape he now resorted to a stratagem.

"Gentlemen," said Tinklepaugh, "don't drown me, please don't. Shoot me if you have determined to kill me, and let my body be buried in the earth instead of in the water, but don't hang me like a felon, or drown me like a cat."

"Hang you like a felon, you miserable negro-loving. South-hater you," answered one of the Klan, "you deserve to be burned like a witch, and to have your ashes thrown in the river as a propitiation to the evil spirit. Or perhaps you would prefer to have your ashes gathered into a tin box and given to the black strumpet you call your wife."

"And is it solely on account of my marriage that you seek to kill me?" asked Tinklepaugh, looking wildly about him as if the truth as to the real cause of his troubles had just flashed into his mind. "I thought it was my political affiliations that gave offense."

"You know better than that," answered the same person who had spoken before; "you know very well that it is on account of your marriage that you are to be punished, and you have been thrice warned of that fact and ordered to leave her."

"I do not deny that I have received warning to desert my wife," answered Tinklepaugh, "but possibly I did not fully understand the true purport of the order and misinterpreted it. I have all the time understood that my politics was the only thing which caused me to be personally disliked, and have thought that the order to abandon my wife was given simply because you did not want to assign the true reason for seeking to banish me from the community, for I cannot see how any objection could be made to my marriage."

"You lie about that," answered the ghoul who had first spoken, giving the rope, which was still fastened to Tinklepaugh's neck, a jerk which nearly threw him off his feet. "You know very well that a white man is not allowed to marry a negro."

"Ah, gentlemen, I see now your mistake," answered Tinklepaugh, with a cunning wink, which could not be discerned in the darkness; "you take me to be a pure blooded white man, but such is not the case. My father was a free negro before the war, and hence there is a mixture of African blood in my veins which makes it not unlawful, but proper, for me to marry a colored woman."

"Can you prove that?" asked the ghoul.

"I will swear it, and can furnish ample proof if given the opportunity."

"Then swear it, and you shall be discharged for the present, and may furnish further proof some other time."

A lantern hung to the pummel of one of the saddles was produced, and the following oath was taken and subscribed, after which Tinklepaugh was discharged and the crowd dispersed:

"I, Peter Tinklepaugh, do solemnly swear that my father was of mixed blood, having been born a free negro before the emancipation of the late slaves, and that I have all my life associated with the colored people, and will continue to do so in the future.

"PETER TINKLEPAUGH."

Sworn to and subscribed before the Cyclop of the Wizard Ghouls.

CHAPTER V.

A VIPER ENTERS.

The excitement, occasioned by the startling discovery of the skeleton remains of Colonel Albert Seaton, had not abated when Donald Weston answered, as request-ed, the invitation of Judge Farwell by making his per-sonal appearance at the Midland Hotel. By recording the first appearance of our quondam friend, Mr. Weston, as having been made at the Midland Hotel, I do not mean to insinuate that Judge Farwell was entirely destitute of the emotions of true friendship, and that he allowed his old school-mate and friend to arrive in the town without showing him the customary courtesy of meet-ing him at the depot. On the contrary, it is but justice toward the judge to chronicle the fact that he met his friend on his arrival at the depot in an open carriage, and received him with every manifestation of the most cordial friendship; but aside from the fact that a few loungers around the hotel looked up from a game of checkers, that at the time absorbed their attention, and made a few commonplace remarks and trite criticisms upon his personal appearance, as he alighted from the carriage on reaching the hotel, no other notice was taken by the citizens of the town of the arrival in their midst of the future prosecuting attorney for the State in that judicial district, and no public demonstration in honor of the embryotic attorney and carpet-bagger statesman was held.

4

Of the ancestry of Donald Weston I know nothing, and as this, like all other stories of the kind, purports to be a true history of all the characters represented, I will not draw on my imagination to supply that for which my destitution of personal knowledge is responsible. I prefer to acknowledge my ignorance rather than to falsify history. It may be that his genealogy might be traced back to some of the Puritan fathers, who came over in the Mayflower, and who afterwards put into execution that same religious intolerance, which they had sought to escape by their immigration to this land of liberty and religious freedom; or it may be that he might have claimed kinship with some of the ancient Scottish Chiefs or Lords, whose chief claim to nobility was based on the fact that they had clansmen enough to steal cattle from their neighbors and then whip them into subjection, when they sought to recapture their stolen property. His parents may have been ever so upright and honorable, and may have enjoyed the distinction of belonging to the highest circles in State, church and society; but still I am constrained to say of them that they perpetrated a great fraud, when they sent their son Donald out in the world and palmed him off on the people as a man.

In personal appearance he was not at all prepossessing, and any unfavorable opinion of him formed on first acquaintance was not likely to be modified or changed on becoming more intimate with him. Still he was not a monster in shape or size. In stature he was rather diminutive, being only about five feet eight inches in height, and weighing only about one hundred and forty pounds; but he had a very large head, keen piercing black eyes and dark complexion and hair, and judging from his high and expansive forehead and general intellectual appearance a phrenologist would have been justifiable in rating him far above the point of mediocrity.

He was sitting with Judge Farwell on the hotel veranda on the second evening after his arrival, when the judge turned to him with the remark:

"Look here, old fellow, how would you like to go out riding this evening and meet my affianced?"

"Your affianced!" replied Weston in astonishment; "you don't mean to say that you have become so much enamored of these Southern girls that you are actually engaged to marry one of them?"

"Oh, yes, I am," answered the judge proudly, "and you will not be so much astonished at my presumption, either, if ever your black orbs encounter her loveliness."

"Oh, well, of course, I will go," said Weston, "especially since she seems to be such a paragon of excellence, but would it not be a little more consistent with the rules of etiquette in polite society for you to first take me to her house and introduce me there?"

"Of course, it would," answered the judge, "but unfortunately for me, I have to meet her clandestinely at present, having been denied entrance to her father's house."

"Ha, ha!" said Weston, with a sardonic smile, "and how does it comport with the dignity of a judge to be holding clandestine meetings with a young girl, when her father forbids him her society at his house?"

"Don't talk to me about dignity in love affairs," said

the judge. " Love scorns dignity, as well as locks and keys, when either interferes to thwart its purposes."

" Very well," said Weston; "if you love the girl, I will grant you the privilege, so far as I am concerned, of communicating with her in any way possible, for love not only scorns dignity and locks and keys, as you suggest, but it also sets at defiance the rules of etiquette and propriety; but still, if I am to be made *particeps criminis* in violating such rules, I think I have a right to know why it is that you have been denied her society at her father's house, and your reason for asking me to meet her clandestinely."

" I will not deny your right to demand my reason for such an extraordinary proposition," answered the judge, "both on account of my unseemly infraction of the rules of propriety and on account of our former intimate relations, but in order to explain it will be necessary for us to take a cursory view of the recent history and present condition of this country. But, first, I will briefly state that my present embarrassment was precipitated by a few of my court decisions, which simply recognized the Constitutional rights and citizenship of the colored race, and were, therefore, unpalatable to the race-hating Ku Klux, among whom is to be numbered my esteemed prospective father-in-law."

" Her father, a Ku-Klux !" interrupted Weston, showing evident signs of indignation; " then I should respect the orders of a Ku-Klux for once by keeping away from his house and shunning the society of his daughter, not through fear of the lawless monster, but to avoid contamination by association with a Ku-Klux or any of his progeny."

"You do us all three injustice," said the judge, manifesting some anger at the hot words of his friend, but restraining a more violent exhibition of wrath, remembering the natural prejudice and consequent ignorance of his friend regarding everything that pertained to the South. "Major Wyland is a member of the Klan, it is true, and a violent opponent of the reconstruction measures adopted by the Republican party, but he is not the lawless monster your imagination would depict him to be, nor has his daughter inherited infection or become contaminated. With him, as with all other Southerners, politics is the Aaron's rod that swallows up everything else, and as all crimes are considered political in their nature, it follows as a necessary concomitant that all virtues are likewise political, and hence when a political crime is committed for which there is no punishment prescribed in the penal code, as for instance the exercise of the right of suffrage by the colored citizen, it is esteemed a virtue to belong to a secret society, which has for its object the disfranchisement of the recently enfranchised negro, and which is simply a secret Star Chamber court where alleged political offenders are tried and convicted in their absence and on *ex parte* testimony.

"But strange as my words may sound to you, the Republican party is responsible for a great deal of the lawlessness that exists in the South, and many good men have joined the Ku-Klux, believing it the only expedient by which they can regain their former prestige and restore the autonomy of the State. Take for instance the case of Major Wyland. At every election

he sees his former slaves, inexperienced and illiterate
as they are, march up to the polls and there exercise
their rights of citizenship by depositing their ballots,
while he, on account of the test oath imposed by Congress, is deprived of this privilege. And there are
thirty thousand others in this State in the same condition. Let Congress pursue a more lenient and conservative course toward the late enemies of the Union; let
the dominant party show a little more of the magnanimity displayed by Grant when he returned the sword
of Lee, and lawless leagues, the last vestige of the rebellion, will disband at once. Understand me, I am
not apologizing for the existence of the Klan nor for
Major Wyland's connection with it. In my opinion
the existence of any secret political organization in a
community is a serious menace to the lives and liberties of the people, and that such an institution ought
not to be tolerated, and as for Major Wyland I seriously apprehend that he was the chief instrument in
prevailing upon the Klan to proscribe me, and to send
me an insulting and threatening warning in regard to
my official conduct."

"And have they actually threatened you with the
fate of a carpet-bagger, too?" asked Weston in astonishment. "I am beginning to think that you have be-
guiled me into this community of cut-throats and midnight assassins simply for the purpose of having me
swing with you."

"Oh, no, it is not so bad as that," answered Judge
Farwell. "I have not been threatened with death, but
have simply been warned that I must not repeat some
of my recent rulings and decisions on the bench; a

warning I need not tell you, I shall certainly ignore, and that, too, in a manner calculated to express my extreme contempt for the authors of such an insult."

"Oh, well, if that is all, I will dismiss all visions of the murderous hobgoblins, or ghouls, I believe you call them, from my mind, and will try and prepare myself to assist you in showing a supreme contempt for their insolent demands as soon as I receive my commission as prosecuting attorney."

"You will find sufficient exercise for all the talents you possess if you wish to successfully prosecute your docket, without troubling yourself to precipitate a quarrel with your antagonists, especially when Major Wyland appears for the defendant."

"What is his plan of attack?"

"Technically speaking, it is the business of the prosecuting attorney to begin the attack, and generally to continue in the attitude of the aggressor throughout all stages of the proceeding; but you will find that he will assume the aggressive quite frequently, and woe to the lawyer who opposes him unprepared when he does. He is a learned and astute lawyer, possesses wonderful and almost inexhaustible resources, and is one of the most skillful and adroit controversialists I have ever seen."

"Very well," said Weston, with a gesture of impatience, beginning to feel a little discomfitted at the thought of meeting such a dexterous opponent on his first appearance in the forum, "your description of the father inclines me to accept your invitation to meet the daughter, so order our horses and let us be going."

Judge Farwell called to Uncle Ben and ordered two

good saddle-horses from the livery stables to be sent to the Midland hotel, an order which Uncle Ben obeyed with his usual promptitude.

The shadows of the trees along the roadside were beginning to lengthen considerably in the sunshine, when the judge and his friend turned into the well-shaded road leading down by the river bank, and the horse ridden by a young lady in advance of them became frightened at the clattering of the hoofs of the horses behind. Minnie Wyland was a skillful and practiced rider, and checking her horse with the reins, she patted his mane with one hand while she looked back to see who was coming. Observing two persons she was just about to conclude that she was destined to be disappointed in not meeting with Judge Farwell, when that gentleman rode forward and asked to be allowed to introduce his friend. By this time they had reached an old mill seat on the river, the mill itself having been burned by the returning Yankee soldiery, in the spring of 1865, and it was hastily agreed that they should alight and spend an hour there, and that the introduction should be given after dismounting.

For the first time Minnie's innate modesty, the chief virtue and ornament of Southern girls, conquered her desire to be in the company of her accepted lover, and as she alighted on a large stone which formed a part of the abutments of an old bridge, which had been suffered to fall into decay on account of the depressed financial condition of the county, and the consequent inability of the county authorities to keep it in proper repair, she showed evident signs of embarrassment. She knew that these meetings with Judge Farwell were contrary to the wishes of her father—in fact, without his knowledge—and, although the meetings were not through any prearrangement, still she was obliged to acknowledge the fact that, in their accustomed rides, they *expected* to meet with each other, for it does not require a written instrument, under hand and seal, to constitute a lover's agreement for a tryst, and she secretly resolved to discontinue the meetings in the future. Her mother had died in her infancy, leaving her an only child, upon whom her father had ever since lavished a double portion of his affection, and, remembering her father's deep aversion for Judge Farwell, she felt it to be her duty to decline further attentions from him, until time and a better understanding of each other's motives should work a reconciliation between the two. She recognized and deprecated the fact that her father's antipathy for the judge was based solely on political differences, and it was because she had esteemed the objection frivolous that she had hitherto permitted the judge to address her without her father's knowledge; but she felt now that she ought to respect her father's wishes, however trivial she considered his objections to her lover, and with a hope that can only be born in desperation, and that, too, in the breast of a woman whose heart is stirred with love for a man whom she regards as true and honorable, and who is the object of that hope, she looked forward to the time when political animosities should cease, when the hateful sound of the terms, "carpet-bagger" and "scalawag" should vanish, and when all men should be respected and honored for their intrinsic worth, regardless of

party affiliations or place of birth; and so, vainly hop-
ing, she determined that this should be the last meeting
with the judge, until such time as they could meet with
her father's consent.

She was in this state of perturbation when Judge
Farwell, not knowing her embarrassment, for she had
not had opportunity to communicate her thoughts to
him, brought forward his friend, and said:

"Miss Minnie, allow me to introduce my friend, Mr.
Weston; Miss Wyland, Mr. Weston."

Weston bowed with the gracefulness of a dancing-
master, and Minnie returned the salutation with the
stately dignity characteristic of her father's family.
She was dressed in a gray riding habit, and although
her face was a little flushed with the thoughts that had
lately disturbed her mind, she maintained a dignified
composure, and looked a perfect picture of health and
beauty. To Donald Weston she appeared a perfect
paragon, The contour of her face was perfectly lovely,
while her figure was equally faultless, in size and proportion.

"I think I have heard Judge Farwell speak of you,"
said Minnie, in a voice so musical that Weston stood
gazing at her in mute admiration, feeling as if her words
were but the sound of the first touch of a musician's
fingers on the strings of a lute, as a prelude to a song
of enchantment.

"Yes, I have often spoken of him to you," said the
judge, seeing the hesitation of his friend. "He and I
were in college together, and became as intimate as our
different natures would allow, though he generally preferred his books to any other society."

"And I have always found my books my most constant friends," said Weston, recovering his self-possession, "and my experience and observation have taught me that very few of them are fickle, or hurtful in their tendency."

"I presume, then, from the tenor of your remark," said Minnie, "that you have been made to experience the fickleness of human friendship, and have sought solace and companionship only where the lines are indellibly stamped without the power of changing?"

"O, I do not mean to acknowledge myself a confirmed misanthrope," answered Weston, a little disconcerted by the construction placed upon his language by Minnie; in fact, I think a book, being the production of some person's brain, is really a part of the writer, and it would seem like a contradiction to say that I enjoy the society of the creation of a human mind while detesting its author."

"I am also fond of my books," answered Minnie, "and I quite agree with you in your estimate of their value ; but I love nature, too, and am fond of the woods, the fields and flowers. Indeed, I like everything except politics."

"Why, I thought that everybody South was a politician, including the women," answered Weston.

"No, indeed, the women of the South are not politicians," said Minnie; "but many of us, on the contrary, have good reason to deprecate the zeal with which the other sex follow the behests of party."

"It seems to me that all good persons ought to deplore the rancor of party strife which now exists in the South," said Weston ; "especially when party zeal leads men to the extent of organizing themselves into bands of midnight assassins."

"I have never heard of the existence of any bands of assassins in the South," answered Minnie. "It is true, we have the Ku-Klux, who sometimes administer justice in a manner not prescribed in our penal codes, but I have yet to hear of their infliction of punishment where it was not richly deserved."

"Then you approve of the existence of the Ku-Klux?"

"No, not exactly," said Minnie. "I think all such secret organizations are dangerous, and their very existence is to be deplored, but when our ignorant colored people are organized into leagues, which threaten the overthrow of our government, it seems to me that the only way to combat the evils threatened is by counter organizations."

"I presume then, when you say that you do not know of any case in which the Ku-Klux have made a mistake, that in your estimation the threat of personal violence against Judge Farwell was justifiable," said Weston.

"Indeed," answered Minnie, evincing for the first time considerable agitation of mind, "I had not heard of any threat of violence against Judge Farwell."

"Yes," said Weston, "I understand from him that the Ku-Klux have warned him that he must not permit colored men to serve as jurors again on pain of being flogged."

"It is true that I have received a note from the hands of the Ku-Klux," said Judge Farwell, "but I attach but little importance to the fact, and am sure I shall not allow it to influence me in the least in my official conduct."

"I am very sorry that the members of any Klan should have been so indiscreet, not to say unjust," said Minnie, "and I must speak to father about this matter, for I am sure that his political prejudices would not allow him to go to the extent of approving such conduct; but I see it is growing late, and think it time for me to return home."

Judge Farwell assisted Minnie to remount, and soon the two were retracing their steps home. Weston returned by an opposite direction, declaring that he was not satisfied with the extent of his ride among such picturesque scenery. He was now in the midst of the most magnificent natural scenery in the State, the swift and lucid mountain stream being on one side and the craggy and gigantic peaks of the mountains on the other, but all the beauty of the natural surroundings was eclipsed by visions of the transcendent beauty of the face and form of Minnie Wyland. It might as well he said of him now that he was not at all sentimental; on the contrary he was cool, calculating and practical in everything, at least such had hitherto been his disposition; but now as he rode along in solitude the image of Minnie Wyland stood constantly before him, and he found himself inquiring whether he really was fool enough to fall in love with a girl at first sight, and repeating the words of an old song:

> "Tell me not that there is need
> Of time for love to grow;
> The hand that strikes to kill indeed
> Despatches at a blow."

He reached the hotel in advance of Judge Farwell, having gone down the river until he struck a road which led into the town by an opposite direction to that taken by the judge and Minnie. As he sat by a window of his room, looking out upon the quiet town as the last glimmering rays of sunshine faded from the house-tops, every scene of the evening recurred to him as if in a dream. Again he stood by the old mill dam and gazed out upon the waters as they poured over the rocks and half rotten timbers that once arrested the waters in their peaceful flow and compelled them to do service in turning the wheels of the mill, and the sounds of the thousand ripples but reminded him of the musical voice that had so enchanted him during the evening. Again he rode among towering peaks or passed under the branches of the huge oaks that grow on the banks of the river, and even the grandeur of the mountains suggested the surpassing beauty by which he had become so enraptured. His heart now responded to the words of the poet:

> " There is nothing gladsome round me,
> Nothing beautiful to see,
> Since thy beauty's spell has bound me
> But is eloquent of thee."

It is true, he felt a little worried over some of the sentiments expressed by Minnie during the conversation with her, especially her quasi approval of the existence of the Ku-Klux organization; but he very charitably attributed this to the influence and teachings of her father, and so absolved her from all blame. He had observed, too, her change of countenance when informed of the indignity offered Judge Farwell by the

Klan, and he inferred from her evident disapproval of
their action in that instance that she was not accustomed to consider their plans as embracing any but the
lower order of society as then constituted in the Union
Leagues; though, had not her language indicated that
such was her idea of the Klan, he might have ascribed
her displeasure to the fact that she was in love with
the object of their attack in that particular instance.

Having finally decided that he was in fact fool
enough, as he expressed it, to fall in love with a girl
at first sight, he was now more perplexed than ever.
Should he inform Judge Farwell of his passion, and
notify him in a manly way that in future he might
consider him a friendly rival? That would be the
more manly and dignified way, no doubt; but how
would Judge Farwell accept and act upon such information? This was the main question that bothered
Weston, for he was purely mercenary in all his actions,
and consulted his own interests to the exclusion of the
welfare of all others. Would a disclosure of his secret
result in their complete estrangement? If so, then it
must not be revealed, because all his hopes of political
advancement depended upon the influence and good
will of the judge, and the honor of jumping at one
bound into such a lucrative and honorable office as the
solicitorship of a whole judicial district was not to be
despised or needlessly lost. It did not take him long to
decide the matter, for selfishness was the predominant
part of his nature, and he was anxious to become one
of the leaders of the party in that section. So he decided to sacrifice his manhood and self-respect to serve
his personal interests.

CHAPTER VI.

PARTISAN JUSTICE.

Parcelling out offices among those politically quali-
fied to receive them (which meant that the applicant
must belong to the Republican party) was an important
part of the policy of reconstruction, as practiced in the
South, and it made but little difference whether the
recipient was a carpet-bagger or a scalawag. All that
was necessary was to find a vacancy, and it was immediately filled by the most available candidate, and if no
vacancy could be discovered by the greedy eye of the
demagogue, and the applicant was likely to prove a
valuable acquisition to the party, an office was generally created for his special benefit. However, in the
case of our good friend, Donald Weston, Esq., the
newly-fledged "twenty dollar attorney," no such usurpation of power was necessary, for as soon as his fealty
to the party had been properly vouched for by Judge
Farwell, Col. Worthen Smith, solicitor for the judicial
district, resigned in his favor, and he was immediately
appointed to the vacant place by the governor.

Immediately upon receiving his commission Weston
set about preparing indictments against the Ku-Klux
with the vigor usually displayed by a novice in any profession. His predecessor, he reasoned, was old and
decrepit, and his mental as well as physical faculties
had been so much impaired by age and infirmity, that
he was incapable of grappling with the situation, and
thus he was afforded an opportunity of proving to the
world that the governor had made no mistake in giving

him the coveted appointment. He would be known as a vigorous and fearless prosecutor, and one whom the Ku-Klux could not intimidate.

He soon discovered, however, that he was not to sail always upon a smooth sea, where everything was serene and lovely, and no opposing obstacle was to be encountered. He found that he was destined to be buffeted and retarded in his voyage to the haven of fame by many waves of perplexity and doubt he had not anticipated; and his embarrassment was none the less painful because the difficulties that beset him were of simple solution. For instance, he spent the whole of the first day of his official life in trying to ascertain the proper title to an indictment against an offending colored brother, who had been so ungrateful, not to say indiscreet, as to declare his intention of voting the Democratic ticket at the approaching election, and who had, therefore, been presented by the grand jury for some of his misdeeds, committed before his defection from the Republican party. He found in the Supreme Court Reports such precedents as the following: "State *v.* Jim, a person of color," "State *v.* Sam, a free negro," "State *v.* Tom, a former slave," and he was in a great quandary to know whether to use some such *discriptio personæ*, or to discard all terms suggestive of the "previous condition of servitude" of the defendant, and indict him simply by his name. To a lawyer of experience, such matters would have given no trouble; but it must be remembered that Weston had entered the profession without the requisite preparation, and he found many little things to puzzle him which might, and ought to, have been avoided by proper training.

5

But the reader need not become alarmed, for fear of being invited into the criminal court, and there compelled to listen to the trial of an indictment against some bloody-handed Ku-Klux, charged with a political murder. To require one to sit all day in such a court room, crowded almost to suffocation, as our criminal courts generally are, and to be jostled and elbowed by impudent negroes, and to be compelled to inhale the offensive odors that arise from their bodies, is a punishment that ought not to be inflicted, if it can be possibly avoided, and I have no disposition to do so in the present instance.   No doubt it would be interesting to know how the newly appointed Solicitor succeeded in his first court, and I would be pleased to give the details of some of his first trials, and tell how Maj. Wyland secured an acquittal for a defendant, whom Weston had indicted as the principal felon, when the evidence showed that he was only an accessory before the fact, and was not present at the commission of the offense; or how another, indicted for perjury, was acquitted because the solicitor rested his case upon the evidence of a single uncorroborated witness, while the law requires the testimony of two witnesses in order to sustain a conviction for that offense—and many other scenes and incidents that occurred during the first few days of his official life, it would be interesting to know ; provided the reader could be placed in a comfortable position to see and hear, during the progress of the trial. But, for fear of offending some sensitive nature, I will proceed to the investigation of a civil case, in which the litigants, especially on one side, are more respectable.

The board of commissioners of West county was composed of two negroes and one "imported statesman" from New Jersey, and they promptly refused payment of the notes given to Colonel Albert Seaton by the county, which were found in the cave in Glen Echo, and Major Wyland as promptly instituted suit, asking for judgment against the county and for a *mandamus* against the board of commissioners to compel them to levy the necessary taxes to liquidate the debt. The case came on for trial at the May term, 1870, of the Superior Court for West county, and a large concourse of people assembled in the court-house to hear the trial, nearly all of them being sympathizers with the cause of the plaintiff.

The court-house in Westville was a model stone structure, situated in the centre of a large square and surrounded by magnificent oaks. The ground was covered with a beautiful coat of grass, and under each tree was one or more seats, or benches, for the accommodation of suitors and witnesses, who generally remained outside until the case in which they were interested was reached, when they would be called at the window by the court crier. The crier at this time was Dick Madison, a negro preacher, who officiated in the court-house during the week, and dispensed "de word ob de Lawd" to an admiring and gullible congregation on Sunday, and whose stentorian tones could be heard for miles around.

Promptly at ten o'clock on the morning of the 20th of May, 1870, Judge Farwell took his seat on the bench of the Superior Court for West county, and directed

the crier to open court in the usual form, which that
sable son of Ham proceeded to do as follows: "Oh,
yes! oh, yes! dis honible co't is now open an' reddy fur
bizness; Gawd save de State an' dis honible co't!"

Those who had failed to notice the ringing of the
court-house bell were aroused by the stentorian voice
of the crier, and came rushing into the court-room at
such a rate that the house was soon densely packed.

The first case appearing on the docket for trial was
entitled: "Albert Seaton, Jr., administrator of Albert
Seaton, Sr , *v.* The Commissioners of West County—
Action for debt." Major Wyland appeared for the
plaintiff, and Donald Weston, Esq., who, by reason of
the prominence given him by his official position and
by reason of the supposition that he "had the ear of
the judge," had become the chief oracle of the party in
that section, was employed by the defendant commissioners to represent the interests of the county.

The complaint was read by Major Wyland, which
alleged in substance that the county was indebted to
the plaintiff's intestate in the sum of six thousand dollars, which money had been loaned the county to procure salt for the starving families of Confederate soldiers, and other destitute persons during the late war;
that the money was duly applied as designed; that the
debt thus created was secured by the notes sued on,
which had been duly signed and delivered by the chairman of the board of county commissioners as required
by law, and that no part of the said notes had ever
been paid.

Weston responded by reading an elaborate demurrer

(all pleadings filed by amateur lawyers are elaborate), the substance of which was that the defendants demurred, because:

1. The court had no jurisdiction of the subject-matter of the action.

2. The complaint did not state facts sufficient to constitute a cause of action, since it appeared from the complaint that the contract sued on was based on an illegal consideration, the money for which the notes were given having been used to aid the rebellion.

Having, under the rules, the right to open and conclude the argument on the demurrer, Weston addressed the court as follows:

"*May it please your Honor:* The question presented for the determination of the court by the complaint and demurrer filed in this case, it seems to me, may be summarized in one leading proposition: Was the debt sued on contracted, directly or indirectly, in aid or support of the rebellion? If so, then the contract is void, as coming within the inhibition of the ordinance of the Convention and the State Constitution. I would call your Honor's attention, first, to the fact that the people of this State, in Convention assembled, solemnly ordained that all debts incurred by the State in aid of the late rebellion, directly or indirectly, are void, and no General Assembly of this State shall have power to assume or provide for the payment of the same or any portion thereof, nor to assume or provide for the payment of any portion of the debts incurred, directly or indirectly, by the late so-called Confederate States. I will read to you further from the Constitution:

" 'No county, city, town, or other municipal corpo-
ration, shall assume or pay, nor shall any tax be levied
or collected for, the payment of any debt, or the interest upon any debt, contracted directly or indirectly in
aid or support of the rebellion.'

" Here, may it please your Honor, the people of this
State, as in all other Southern States, have solemnly
declared, through their highest law-making power, that
no debt contracted in aid or support of the rebellion
shall be recognized as valid, and this declaration of the
will of the people is obligatory upon the courts. So,
now, recurring to the proposition I at first announced:
Was furnishing salt to the people during the war a measure calculated and intended to aid the rebellion? As
counsel for the defendants, it becomes my duty, in argu
ing the demurrer, to maintain the affirmative of this
issue; and, in doing so, I wish to inquire, first, what
relation the county of West sustained towards the rightful government of the State at the time this contract
was made? It is a fact, of which this court is bound to
take judicial notice, that at the date of this contract,
the persons exercising the power of the State, and the
persons exercising the power of West county, had dis-
avowed their allegiance to the government of the United
States and to the rightful State government, and had
assumed an attitude of open hostility to the rightful
State government and to the United States government.
There was rebellion in the State, and the spirit of rebellion reigned supreme. It follows, therefore, that this
court, which simply exercises the functions and powers
of the rightful State government after regaining its

supremacy, cannot treat the acts and contracts of persons so unlawfully exercising the powers of the State and county authority as valid, unless the court is satisfied that the acts were innocent, and such as the lawful government would have done. In this case the plaintiff is asking the court to compel the present county commissioners, who are in the rightful exercise of the power of the county, to perform a contract made by a set of men who were wrongfully pretending to act as commissioners and exercise the power of the county in 1862. Any act which would not have been done except for the existence of the rebellion, and which was calculated to counteract the measures adopted by the government of the United States for its suppression, and to enable the people in insurrection to protract the unholy struggle, was in aid of the rebellion. Furnishing salt for the use of the women and children at home, was clearly calculated to counteract the blockade and other measures resorted to by the United States to suppress the rebellion ; because the rebels in arms were thereby relieved of the duty of laying down their arms, and returning to the support of those for whose subsistence they were responsible, and were enabled thereby to protract the struggle ; and the plea that the women and children were in a state of actual starvation, and that the motive in contracting the debt was to do an act of charity and humanity, and mitigate the rigors of war, is but a simple confession of the illegality of the contract ; because the laws of war are paramount to motives of charity and humanity, and starving the women and children was a legitimate means, adopted by the rightful government, to compel the rebel authorities to surrender."

Maj. Wyland listened to the above argument, especially to the closing sentences, with real anguish of heart,
but every exhibition of feeling or passion was suppressed
with the iron will of a Stoic. On the street, he probably
would have resented the avowal of the monstrous proposition that starving innocent women and children was a
legitimate means of terminating a war; but in the court-
house he was nothing but a lawyer—cool, careful, and
deliberate—and every passion, or thought, that was
calculated to becloud his mental vision, or detract, in
any way, from his reasoning powers, was banished at
once. He knew that the legal attainments of his antag
onist were very limited, and that he was inexperienced,
and he had observed, also, that Weston had cited no
authorities to sustain the position he had assumed; but
still he recognized the strong native ability of his opponent, and realized the fact that, with the evident prejudice of the presiding judge against him, he had a fight
on his hands that required skillful argument, supported
by an abundant array of authorities and precedents.
As he arose to address the court, in reply, he glanced
at Weston, and made toward him a peculiar gesture,
indicative of displeasure, which he habitually did when
aroused to indignation; but that eminent worthy simply assumed a more defiant attitude, and looked more
than ever like a cabbage, all head and no body, while
a smile of anticipated triumph played over his features.
Maj. Wyland said:

"*May it please your Honor:* I have listened to the
argument of the counsel for the defendant in this case

with that degree of interest and attention which a legal argument always elicits from me, especially when I know it to be my duty to oppose the application of the principles of law sought to be enforced; but I must confess that the avowal of such a monstrous proposition of law as that feeding the non-combatant, starving and helpless women and children, in a time of war, is aiding the rebellion in such a sense as to make void a contract for food furnished them, is a declaration of a doctrine that is unwarranted by authority, and one that the moral sentiment of mankind can never approve, nor the courts enforce, without contravening all the traditions and history of free government, and crushing the very genius of liberty itself. The complaint in this case states that the contract was made in a time of great scarcity; that the destitution of the people was such that they could not procure salt, and that they had, in many instances, been reduced to the necessity of digging up the dirt under their meat houses and boiling it, to extract the salt which the earth had absorbed. The legal effect of a demurrer is to admit the truth of all the facts stated in the complaint; so, then, the motive, as appears by the facts admitted, was not war, but simply to supply the urgent wants of our nature.

"But I am aware, your Honor, that the moral aspect of this case is not to be allowed to dictate the opinion of the court, and I, therefore, plant myself squarely on the law, and insist that, by a strict construction of the principle of law involved, the plaintiff is entitled to recover.

"A preliminary question is: What was the relation

between the State and the United States when this contract was made?

" In *Thorington* v. *Smith*, 8 Wall., 1, it is settled that it was a *de facto* government, and that its *civil* administration was lawful, and it was the *duty* of the citizens to observe the laws of a peaceful character. ·

"In *U. S.* v. *Rice*, 4 Wheat., 246, and in *U. S.* v. *Howard*, 2 Gall., 485, and in *Wheat. Int. Nat. Law*, 337, 345 and 346, it is held that the conquest and military occupation of part of our territory by the public enemy makes it foreign territory, and subject to the laws arising out of that relation.

" In the *Surah Starr. Bl. Prize cases*, 69, it is settled that, for all purposes of the war, it was a war with a foreign power, and involved all the consequences of international wars.

"In the cases of the *Union Ins. Co.* v. *U. S.*, 6 Wall., 759, and *Armstrong's Foundry*, 6 Wall., 766, it is decided that the laws of *capture and prize* apply to the acts of confiscation of rebel property—otherwise, *the law of nations.*

" And in *Shank's* v. *Dupont*, 3 Pet., 260, it is held that the relation between the body politic and its members continues the same, notwithstanding a change of government.

" I. From these authorities are deduced clearly these conclusions :

" 1. That we had a civil government in this State competent to enact all civil laws not belligerent to the United States.

" 2. And that the law of nations governed the conduct of the war between the State and the United States.

" 3. They establish this further principle, if our case required it—that the law of nations, which is part of the common law, is as obligatory upon a nation dealing with its own subjects as with foreign nations.

" II. The second proposition, and main one, is, that this contract is not forbidden by the law of nations, or the law which governs a nation at war with its own subjects, in a state of rebellion of the magnitude and acknowledged character of this.

" The uniform decisions of the courts of all nations for many ages, and the writings of eminent jurists, have settled what acts and things constitute that 'aid to a war', which is forbidden, so as to become the subject of judicial cognizance. If two nations go to war, it is the duty of all others to stand off, and furnish no aid to either. If, however, the subjects of another government do furnish supplies *calculated and intended to aid one party in the prosecution of the war*, these supplies are called '*contraband of war*,' and become the subject of capture and prize.

" The term *contraband*, then, embraces, and was intended to embrace, every act or thing which is in 'aid of' a war or rebellion, in a legal sense.

" What, then, is *contraband of war?*

" All merchandise is divided into three classes:

" 1. Articles manufactured and primarily and exclusively used for military purposes in time of war.

" 2. Articles which may be, and are, used for purposes of war or peace, according to circumstances.

" 3. Articles exclusively used for peaceful purposes.

" *Provisions* belong to the second class, and is our case.

As to these, the rule is that they are contraband only when *actually* destined to the military or naval use of the belligerents. *Wheaton Int. Nat. Law*, pp. 376–381; 1 *Kent Com.*, pp. 134–41; *The Peterhoff*, 5 Wall., 58.

" From these cases and the text-books is clearly derived this proposition—that salt is never contraband or in aid of war unless *actually* destined to the military use of the belligerents, as to a *besieged place, or the army.* In our case the facts are that the salt was sent to and used only by the women and children at home.

" Take the case of *Leak* v. *Commissioners of Richmond County*, 64 N. C., 132: Grant intercepts provisions going into Vicksburg, *a besieged town.* They are clearly contraband. But if Vicksburg had not been beseiged, and no hostile army there, it is equally clear they would not be contraband.

" It is established, then, that the purchase of salt for the people of the county was an act lawful and innocent in itself; and he who affirms the contrary must show it. We do not rest our case here, as we might, but assume the affirmative of establishing our innocence in fact.

" The Acts of Assembly are divisible into two classes: 1. Those *in aid of the war*, which are void. 2. Those of *civil administration*, which are valid, as settled in *Thorington* v. *Smith*. Note the facts in detail.

" 1. It is 'an act for the supply of salt' and confined to that one purpose of distribution among the *home* people, without any reference to a military purpose.

" 2. No act touching military supplies was passed in reference to it.

" 3. The legislature observed the distinction between acts of a military and civil nature, and the captions so designate them generally, or the body of the act does. So much for the legislature. Now as to the county :

" 1. The county is not sovereign, and has only limited delegated powers. Being a mere subordinate agent, the agent may be innocent, although the principal is guilty. Here all the facts establish the *unwarlike* and innocent purpose of the county.

" 2. The loan was made twelve months after the act, under the pressure of necessity, 'great scarcity, and the people were in great need of salt', the case states. The motive, then, was not war; but to supply the urgent wants of our nature.

" 3. The most scrupulous provision was made to secure an equal and uniform distribution among all, black and white, at home, thus rebutting all hostile purpose.

" 4. The county passed '*no act of secession*', no 'series of war measures', but was a subordinate fraction of the State, and bound, willing or not, to obey; and without power to resist the State.

" But the *county* might be guilty and the plaintiff not.

" 1. His act was involuntary; the county went to him to borrow.

" 2. The county agent merely stated to him that he wanted the salt for the people of the county—a non-military purpose.

" 4. No guilty knowledge of an unlawful purpose on his part is shown. He was not bound to know a *void* act of the legislature, and no actual notice is proved.

" 5. Finally the claim is audited, and allowed by the county court, in 1867.

"Then, why should not this debt be paid? If a famine had occurred in time of peace (and history is full of instances) a civil government which folded its hands, stood aloof and said to the sufferers, 'perish!' would have been looked upon by all mankind with horror and detestation. Is the duty less sacred, because the famine is in consequence of war and rebellion, and the government is *de facto* and not *de jure?*

"The distinction, as I have already said, is one that the moral sentiment of mankind can never approve, and is unwarranted by authority. The doctrine of what is 'aid to rebellion' may be carried to such an extent that our courts will become a means of oppression, instead of a place to which the injured may resort for the enforcement of his rights. Such an error, I am sure, this court would wish to avoid."

When Major Wyland closed his argument, the audience, nearly all of whom had sympathized with the cause of the plaintiff from the beginning, gave evident signs of approval, and a subdued whisper pervaded the whole court-room. Weston arose to reply, but Judge Farwell, who well knew the inability of his friend to combat the legal points presented by Maj. Wyland, motioned for silence and said:

"I think it altogether unnecessary to protract the argument in this case further. It is conceded in the authorities cited by the counsel for the plaintiff that, in case of a blockade, an attempt to introduce salt or other provisions violates the law of nations, and the articles are lawful prizes, for the reason that by the blockade it is proclaimed to the world that starvation is resorted to as one of the means of compelling peace, and, this being recognized by the law of nations as one of the means that a belligerent may resort to, any one venturing to run the blockade does so at his peril. Now, it is a historical fact, of which the court may take judicial notice, that the late war was conducted on a scale of magnificent proportions. The whole South was in a state of seige at the time the contract sued on was made—a blockade and military possession of ports on the east and south! arms on the north and west! It is, therefore, the opinion of this court that the manufacture and distribution of salt by the wrongful authorities in possession of the State government, and the wrongful county authorities, was in contravention of the avowed policy of the government of the United States, and in aid of the rebellion, as tending to protract the struggle; and that money loaned to the county in order to procure salt for the use of soldiers' families, and other destitute persons, cannot be recovered. Judgment will therefore be entered for the defendant commissioners, and against the plaintiff."*

On the announcement of the decision of the court, Albert Seaton sat for a moment, stupefied with astonishment, and then buried his face in his hands in a paroxysm of despair. How could he inform his invalid mother of the disastrous termination of the suit? Only a few days before, he had induced her to sign with him a mortgage on the old homestead, to enable him to purchase the out-

---

*The author pleads guilty to the charge of plagiarism in this chapter, having quoted largely from the opinion in *State* v. *Commissioners*, 64 N. C. Rep., 516, and from the brief filed by the counsel for plaintiff in that case.

of the *Westville Conservative*, and he had just entered upon his editorial duties with a high hope of being able to liquidate the mortgage at once with the proceeds of the suit, but now all his hopes had been dashed to the ground with one blow, and the dear old homestead would be obliged to be sold.

Albert was sitting in this posture when Major Wyland approached, and touching him gently on the shoulder, said, "Arise, my boy, and let us us go home. We have no further business here. When our courts of justice are prostituted to the service of partisan hatred, and our judges view everything through the green goggles of prejudice, our rights are no longer protected, and it is useless to seek an enforcement of them in court." The irate old lawyer spoke with much feeling, and exhibited, for the first time during the day, evidences of the strong and rankling passions that were tearing his breast.

As Albert turned to take the arm of his counsel and leave the court-room, he cast an appealing look at Judge Farwell, but that dignitary met his glance with averted face, and directed his sable assistant, the crier, to adjourn court for the day.

Major Wyland and Albert went directly from the court-house to the home of Major Wyland, where they found Minnie and Albert's sister, Bessie, waiting to learn the result of the suit. The Wyland residence was a magnificent stone structure, situated on a commanding eminence in the suburbs of the town, and was surrounded by large and beautiful magnolias and other evergreens. The place exhibited no signs of dilapidation and ruin, the usual painful remembrances of the vanished fortunes of Southern aristocracy; for as late as the year 1870, many of our blue-blooded aristocrats were still gnawing the bones of an *ante-bellum* wealth that dissolved before the sunlight of emancipation But everything about the premises showed evidences of a luxuriant prosperity.

As Albert entered the large folding-door of the mansion, his sister met him, eager to hear the news; but his haggard appearance told the story at once. "Oh, my brother," she sobbed, "I see it is useless to ask you the termination of the case; the pallor of disappointment is on your face."

The agitation of his sister nerved him to make a brave reply, for a true man always becomes stronger at the sight of helplessness around him. "Never mind, my sister," said Albert, "the case is not hopelessly lost yet, for we have the right of appeal to the Supreme Court, and it may be that the appellate court will interpret the law differently, and the right may yet prevail."

"I am sorry to say that I do not feel very confident of success before the Supreme Court," interposed Maj. Wyland; "for I have observed with extreme regret the partisan bias manifested by that court recently, and they have already decided, adversely to the claimants, questions of a similar character to that presented by the case to-day. Indeed, the active participation of the members of that court in political affairs has attracted the attention of members of the bar throughout the State; and so deep have they descended into the depths of partisan mire that the lawyers who prac-

6

tice before the court, or at least a large number of them,
have felt it to be their imperative duty, in order to preserve the dignity of that tribunal, to publish a solemn
protest against their participation in political struggles."

" Yes," answered Albert, "and I believe those same
lawyers have been punished for their alleged imperti-
nence by being attached for contempt and deprived of
the privilege of appearing before the court until they
purge themselves of the contempt."

"And they may wait for an answer to their rule to
show cause why I should not be attached for contempt
until the devil summons *them* to answer for their own
real sins," answered the old lawyer defiantly. "I signed
the protest, because I deprecated the action of our Supreme Court judges in entering the campaign, and I
would suffer my tongue to rot in the palate of my
mouth before I would utter one word of excuse for my
action, and I would let my right arm become palsied
by inaction before I would sign any answer disavowing
my contempt."

"But tell me, father," said Minnie, "why Judge Farwell decided against you to-day. I thought you were
confident of success this morning."

"Because he is a miserable time-server and demagogue, instead of an impartial judge," answered the
major roughly.

"But surely he could not decide the matter arbitrarily
and without any authority or reason to support his
opinion," said Bessie, as she took her seat on the sofa
beside Minnie and placed her arm tenderly around her
waist. She knew that Minnie loved the judge, and she
saw how the harsh words of Maj. Wyland had wounded

her heart, and she hastened to sustain and comfort her with a woman's sympathy.

"I know of no authority in law, reason, or humanity to sustain, or even justify, his decision," answered the major.

"Father," said Minnie in a voice almost choked with emotion, "I cannot believe that Judge Farwell would do any one the injustice to arbitrarily refuse to grant relief in a case of that kind. He surely could have no motive for doing Albert an injury."

"Motive," answered her father indignantly; "there was motive enough to my mind. His object was to pander to the prejudices of radical reconstructionists, and in order to do so he was willing to prostitute our courts of justice to serve base party purposes, while other scapegrace carpet-baggers and scalawags rob and impoverish the State and try to make us bear our humiliation without murmuring."

"Oh, papa, don't speak so harshly," said Minnie, as she laid her head on Bessie's shoulder and sobbed audibly and bitterly. "Be charitable enough, at least toward me, to assign some reason for his action."

"Then I will give you the only reason assigned by himself for his decision while on the bench," said the major. "He based his opinion on the principle that the whole South during the war was in a state of seige, and that even articles of provision furnished the beseiged became contraband of war, and on that principle he decided that money loaned for the purpose of procuring salt for starving women and children at home could not be recovered in court. And I tell you, Min-

nie, and I say it emphatically and authoritatively, that
any man who entertains such an opinion as that is not
worthy of the hand of any Southern girl, who loves
her country and cherishes its history and traditions."

At this Minnie commenced crying, and Albert and
Bessie, seeing how embarrassing the situation was becoming, bade their friends good evening, and returned
home to go through the same scene of weeping with
their invalid mother.

Tears are women's weapons, and are the most eloquent and persuasive arguments that can be produced.
At the sight of his daughter lying prostrate and in tears
on the sofa, the stern father relented, at least to such
an extent that he folded her in his arms, and, stroking
her fevered forehead gently with his hand, said : " My
daughter, I did not wish to wound your heart unneces-
sarily. You may think me stern and inflexible when
I ought to be more indulgent, but I want to re-assure
you that my harshest treatment is from a father's love
and consideration for your future happiness. I have
an inveterate hatred for the man you have chosen to be
your future husband, and his decision to-day shows him
to be so utterly destitute of all human sympathy that I
regard him as more of a monster than ever. I think
his judgment in that case to-day a disgrace to the judiciary of our State. But let us not talk more of this
matter now. I am satisfied that future events will vindicate my course, and convince you that it would be
supreme folly to entrust your happiness to the keeping
of one who disregards the ties of common humanity
and justice.

" Now retire to your room, my darling, and dry your tears, and don't think your father cruel. Ever since the day you were born, I have loved you as my only offspring, and ever since the death of your dear mother, I have bestowed upon you the undivided affections of my heart. Listen to me, my sweet child," and the father patted his daughter on her cheeks and wiped away her tears with his handkerchief as he spoke: " There is no wish of your heart but that shall be gratified, if I can only be convinced that to grant it will not endanger your future welfare; and I promise you now that if future events shall convince me that I have misjudged him whom you love, I will make every reparation in my power, and not a single desire of yours shall ever be thwarted by any intervention on my part. Go to bed, darling, and you shall yet be happy. Good night."

The old lawyer kissed his daughter affectionately, as he bade her good night, and Minnie retired to her room. The father repaired to his study, and again he was only a lawyer, utterly destitute of all sympathy or affection, and totally oblivious of everything unconnected with the legal question that for hours absorbed his attention.

CHAPTER VII.

LOVE OR GOLD?

On the morning after the trial of the famous salt case,
Donald Weston sat in his room at the Midland hotel,
wrapped in profound meditation.   He was in a quandary, and this was it: He was desperately in love with
Minnie Wyland, but at the same time he was terribly
infatuated with the schemes of public plunder inaugu-
rated by the solons of the "grip-sack party," and he
was constantly beset by the alluring temptation to stuff
his grip-sack with gold and the fraudulent tax bonds,
which the political cormorants at the State Capital had
caused to be issued; but he knew he could not win
both, and that if he ever expected to possess Minnie
Wyland as a wife, he would have to sever his connection with the Republican party, and give up all hope
of further political preferment and of accumulating
riches by the nefarious schemes practiced around him.
To seek to win the hand of Minnie would make him
guilty of treason and ingratitude toward his friend and
benefactor, whom he knew to be her affianced; to enter
into the saturnalia of public plunder and financial de-
bauchery, then being carried on about him, would make
him guilty of treason and theft as against the State, for
he was well aware of the fraudulent character of the
bonds issued.   His conscience was flexible enough to
permit him to do either, without being harassed with
any compunction ; and so, his conscience being easy, he

simply sat and weighed in his mind the two passions
of love and greed, and waited to see which would con-
quer in the struggle. And yet he was not altogether
like a ship, plunged in turbulent waters without a rudder. The astuteness of his powerful mind, which never
deserted him, was stronger than any malady that ran-
kled in his heart; and reason, untrammelled by conscience and influenced solely by selfish motives, became
the rudder to guide his course through the agitated
waters.

Minnie Wyland, he reasoned, was an only child, and
her father was already immensely rich, having wisely
invested all his accumulations before the war in real
estate, instead of following the popular method of investing in human chattels; and, besides, he had a large and
lucrative practice as an attorney, and a conjugal partnership with the daughter and only heir and a business
partnership with the old man, could not be considered
a very hazardous and foolish venture. Besides, he was
not altogether certain that the carnival of crime and
political corruption, practiced by the dominant party,
would go always unpunished; or that the Republican
party would remain always in power, though he was
fully cognizant of the fact that a gigantic conspiracy
had been concocted, by the Governor and his unscrupulous coadjutors in this State and at Washington City,
to perpetuate the reign of that party by the aid of
Federal bayonets and the State militia.

He had frequently visited Minnie at her home since
his first meeting with her at the ruins of the old mill
on the river, having become the principal means of

communication between her and her banished lover ; and
he had so often hinted his unbounded admiration for
her that he felt sure the declaration of love, which he
finally decided to make that evening and so settle the
question whether in the future he should continue to
be a faithless friend or political miscreant, would not
so startle her that he would be unable to obtain, at
least, a respectful hearing. The crafty little demagogue had so far pursued a very conservative course
in all matters relating to the public for the sole purpose of ingratiating himself into the good graces of
Minnie and her father, and in order to quietly supplant
Judge Farwell in the affections of his betrothed ; but
he knew that the sentiments, expressed by him on the
trial the preceding day, would have a tendency to in-
jure him in the estimation of the " Bourbon element,"
as the faction to which Major Wyland belonged was
called, and it was this reflection that caused him to
resolve to act so precipitately in declaring his love.
If he should be successful in his suit, he would resign
his office as prosecuting attorney for that district and
repudiate the Republican party forever ; if he should
be discarded, he would be ready to plunge at once into
the wildest excesses of extravagance—thievery and
scoundrelism that then reveled in the State—and swim
with the tide. He felt that Major Wyland was too
much of a lawyer himself not to reserve for him the
charitable thought that the sentiments he expressed
on the trial of the salt case might not have emanated
from the heart, but were possibly the feigned sentiments of a lawyer, resorted to for the purpose of gain-

ing his case, and he hoped to be able to satisfy Minnie with the same explanation.

Having resolved to turn patriot and repudiate the party of corruption and thievery, on condition that Minnie should accept him as a lover and discard Judge Farwell (the condition was quite apposite since patriotism, as Dr. Johnson observes, is the last refuge of a scoundrel), he proceeded, as soon as evening approached, to wend his way toward the object of his passion, determined to make one desperate effort to win her hand, though he knew that in so doing he was flinging away forever the friendship and respect of the friend of his youth and benefactor of his manhood years on the bare risk of success.

He found Minnie sitting on a rustic seat, under a large elm in one corner of the yard, looking more disconsolate than he had ever seen her. She held a book in her hand and pretended to be reading, but her swollen eyes and troubled appearance in general showed too plainly that her thoughts were not on the book. Weston had observed the haggard expression on her countenance before she discovered his presence, and shrewdly divined the cause, and when she looked up and he saw on her face an expression of relief, his heart bounded with a hope it had never before known. It showed that she was glad to see him, at least.

"Good evening, Miss Minnie," he said, bowing politely; "I am very glad to find you out in the open air this beautiful evening. I hope your mind is as tranquil and your heart as light as the gentle zephyrs around you."

"Good evening, Mr. Weston," answered Minnie, rising and bowing with her accustomed grace; "I am sorry to say that I do not enjoy, this evening, that happy state of mind and heart your kindness would wish for me; but it may be that you will be able to tranquilize my mind and make my heart beat in consonance with the peaceful scenery around me. Pray be seated."

"I am sure, it would afford me much pleasure to be able to assist you in securing all the happiness that the most favored existence can afford," said Weston, taking a seat beside her. He wanted to say, further, that the object of his visit was to offer her just such a state of ecstatic bliss, but he feared to be too precipitate.

"I am satisfied from the favors you have formerly shown me," answered Minnie, "that you would do all in your power to add to my happiness. You know that at the suggestion of Judge Farwell, I have given you my confidence, and in many instances I have treated you as a confidential friend and adviser, and it is in regard to him that I wish to speak with you this evening."

"And what is it you want to know about him?"

"Oh, I want to know all about the trial yesterday," answered Minnie, speaking earnestly. "Papa says it is a disgrace to the whole judiciary of the State."

"I cannot agree with your father, that other judges are to be held responsible for one man's mistakes," he answered; "but I must confess that, in my estimation, the decision is one that will not add any lustre to Judge Farwell's fame as a judge."

"Then you really think he did wrong?" asked Min-

nie, vainly trying to suppress a tear that scalded her
eyelid. "Ought we not to be charitable enough to say
that it was probably a mistake, and not a wilful per-
version of justice?"

" I would very gladly give him credit for simply making a mistake," Weston answered ; "but my knowledge
of the true facts compels the admission that, in my
opinion, he was simply carrying out the policy dictated
by the governor, which is to humiliate all those who
adhere to the Conservative or Democratic party, and
to drive them, by whatever means, into the Republcan
party."

"And what are the facts which justify such an opinion?" asked Minnie, still clinging to her affianced and
vainly trying to defend his actions against the artful
wiles of the wretch by her side.

"Why, simply that we discussed the case together
before the trial came on," answered Weston ; "and I
know his sentiments and true judgment on the questions involved. He intimated to me that such would
be his decision when the action was first instituted,
and before I filed my demurrer. I protested against
filing such a demurrer for a long time ; but my clients,
the county commissioners, were aware of his opinion,
and I was forced to succumb in deference to their
wishes, or give up the case after having been retained
by the payment of a fee. Besides, I was inexperienced
myself, and had great respect for, and confidence in,
Judge Farwell's judgment until I heard the masterful
argument of your father."

The villian knew all this was a lie, but he had set

out with the purpose of doing all the lying necessary to accomplish his object, and he knew that Minnie's confidence in the judge would be very much shaken by such statements from one whom she trusted as his friend as well as hers.

Minnie sighed deeply, and for a few moments neither spoke. The one was weighing in her mind all the charges she had heard in regard to Judge Farwell, against the many excellent qualities she knew he possessed; while the other was considering, cautiously, to what extend he should attempt to poison her mind against the judge before declaring his own love. At last Weston broke the silence.

"I assure you, Miss Minnie, that it grieves me, as much as you, to have my faith shaken in the man whom I have respected and admired since my early youth. It has pained me very much lately to observe his tendency toward the extreme partisan measures inflicted upon the people by the demagogues and unprincipled adventurers now in power in this State. I have often admonished him of this evil inclination, and have frequently warned him that his membership in the Union League would prove to be the rock upon which his political fortunes would be wrecked."

"Oh, do not tell me he belongs to the detestable Union League," said Minnie, shuddering at the thought.

"Yes, I feel it my duty to inform you of these facts," answered the serpent, "because I would not wish to appear as responsible for any deception as to his true character that might be practiced upon you. I have several times sought the opportunity of making this disclosure, but have been deterred from doing so by a friendly consideration for your own feelings."

"I appreciate your kindness," she answered. "You were very considerate to think of my happiness at all."

"I assure you I have thought of nothing else lately," said the wily serpent. "Indeed, if my mind should follow the inclination of my heart, my only thought would be that your happiness was inseparably connected with my own."

"I do not think I comprehend your meaning," she answered.

Weston saw that the supreme moment of his life had arrived, and he nerved himself for the ordeal.

"I mean simply," he answered, and his voice trembled with real emotion, "that I love you, myself, and my highest ambition is to have you reciprocate that feeling."

Minnie cast her eyes upon the ground, and restlessly turned the leaves of her book.

"I am surprised at you, Mr. Weston," she answered at last. "I had not thought of such a thing."

"Indeed, I know you have not," he answered; "but still, I have been burning to tell you of my love for several days. I have governed my passion with the heroism of a Stoic, and have bided the time, which I knew would come, when the true character of your accepted lover would be disclosed to you, and you would be ready to hear my own story, without accusing me of faithlessness toward Judge Farwell, and without the necessity, on my part, of appearing as his rival."

"I have not yet discarded Judge Farwell," answered

Minnie, decidedly, "though I must confess that the
events of yesterday, and the facts you have related to
me this evening, have rudely shaken my plighted faith.
Still, the vows of love are not to be ruthlessly broken."

"Nor the offerings of love to be ruthlessly trampled
upon," answered Weston, while the burning passion of
his soul beamed eloquently through his piercing black
eyes.

"Oh, do not speak to me of this matter now," she
said ; "my heart is already broken."

"Then it ought to be the more accessible," he answered.

"You are mistaken," she answered ; "the rent heart
only asks for time to heal."

"Is not love the only balm for a wounded heart?"

"Yes, I believe it is."

"Then accept my love, and do not torture me longer.
Oh, Minnie," he said, rising and looking her full in the
face, while his tremulous voice and passionate eyes
told beyond dispute the genuineness and depth of his
love, "I love you with all the ardor of my burning
soul! I throw my life and future happiness at your
feet! Do not despise me! Love me! Be my wife, and
I will rob heaven itself of its sweetest comforts to make
you happy!"

"Mr. Weston," answered Minnie, after a few moments
spent in deep reflection, "I think a man pays a woman
the highest compliment possible when he offers her his
love and asks her to be his wife. I am sure I appreciate the compliment you have paid me, but——."

"Please do not tell me you appreciate it only as a
compliment," interrupted Weston eagerly. "Love only

is the return for love. All else is emptiness to the heart that offers love. Do not dismiss me in that way. Only tell me you will consider the matter. It may be that I have been too precipitate. Give me but a ray of hope, and Cupid himself shall lend it effulgence."

"I am sorry, Mr. Weston," and the girl spoke calmly now, "but my love is forever pledged to another. It may be that I have been deceived in him, and that he is not the honorable and upright gentleman I have esteemed him to be. If so, then my heart is sealed against the love of all men forever. I cannot love another."

"Then you reject my suit, and spurn the offer of my love?"

"Do not say 'reject' and 'spurn,'" said Minnie: "those are harsh words, and I did not apply them. Say, rather, that my heart is another's until time shall reveal his true character, at least, and that I cannot love another even though I should cease to love him."

"And I do not even have your permission to renew my plea, but must regard your decision to-day as final?"

"Yes, as final," but the girl spoke kindly, and there was the sound of compassion in her voice.

"Then I leave you ; but remember, proud girl, that I shall return to you again," and the wily, creeping, cringing, fawning, wiry serpent began to hiss at the object of his passion. "And if I do return, it will be as the villain of villains, and your circumstances will then be such that you may be ready to accept the proffered hand of the villain and be free!"

"Mr. Weston," said Minnie, rising and trembling violently with fear, "your language appalls and frightens

me. I cannot imagine how I have so incurred your displeasure, and am sure I meant you no injury. I do not
see why our friendship should be changed into the
deadly enmity you threaten me with, simply because
I tell you I cannot love you."

"Friendship!" echoed the enraged little man in a
fury of passion. "And I will yet change that friendship into love, or I will make the very remembrance of
it a canker in your brain that will drive you to distrac-
tion!"

Minnie now became seriously alarmed, and retreated
hastily toward the house, leaving the baffled and rejected little demon alone in the yard.

As soon as Weston recovered from the blindness of
his fury, he walked back to his hotel, and entering his
room he unlocked his trunk and unfolded his commission as solicitor for the judicial district.

"This," said he, holding it proudly and defiantly
above his head, "is the emblem of my authority and
the weapon of my power. By this weapon I will smite
to the ground every barrier that impedes me in my
career toward fame and wealth, *or*," and he clenched
his fists and fairly hissed the words, "*that opposes my
marriage with Minnie Wyland!*"

CHAPTER VIII.

TWO VILLAINS MEET.

It was on a beautiful afternoon in June, 1870, and not many days after the events recorded in the last chapter, when Donald Weston alighted from a carriage in front of a log school-house. In this unpretentious little building Peter Tinklepaugh, the mixed-blooded little pedagogue, with whom we formed an acquaintance in a former chapter,

"————— reared the hickory sprout,
And taught the little black urchins how to shout."

On the announcement of Weston's appearance at the door, Tinklepaugh went forward to meet him with a bland smile, and his little villainous heart was filled with as much genuine joy as that little receptacle of so many wicked designs could possibly hold. He gave the hand of his visitor a cordial grasp, and invited him in the house, with many assurances of his pleasure at meeting him, and of his appreciation of the honor of receiving a visit from so distinguished a personage.

"I am very glad to make your acquaintance, Mr. Tinklepaugh," said Weston, as he advanced to the proffered seat on one of the rude benches next to the log wall, which had been speedily vacated in his honor.

"I hope you will make yourself as comfortable as our meagre accommodations will allow, while we finish the few remaining exercises of the evening," said Mr. Tinklepaugh.

7

"Do not let me interrupt your work," answered
Weston, "and I assure you I will be quite comfortable
here by this window. I have no doubt, too, that I
will enjoy listening to the exercises of your pupils,
and witnessing the advancement made by them since
their emancipation."

"I am sorry to say that we are so seldom honored
by the appearance of a visitor at this institution that
we have made very little preparation for the entertain-
ment of others," answered Peter. "However, we will
do the best we can, and I hope our faults will be over-
looked out of charity."

"I assure you I fully appreciate the many difficulties
you have to encounter," answered Weston, "and I desire, also, to be allowed to pay you the high compliment
of attesting the appreciation of your friends of the
fact that you possess bravery enough to defy popular
prejudice and pursue your present occupation."

"No one has felt more keenly than I the extent and
bitterness of that prejudice," answered Tinklepaugh.
"I have been scourged and whipped, threatened with
death, and actually shot at by the murderous Ku-Klux,
until I feel that my life is in danger."

"I wonder that you have the courage to pursue your
avocation in the face of such danger," said Weston.

"Ought a father to refuse bread to his children?
Ought a patriot to remain idle, simply because his path
is beset by dangers, when he sees so much illiteracy
around him, and that, too, among those lately raised
to the rights of citizenship and the dignity of sover-
eigns? We have taken the shackles of slavery from

their feet, and in so doing we were shot at and pierced and butchered, and many of our brave brothers slaughtered on the field of battle; and shall we now refuse to lift the manacles of a deadlier slavery from their minds, simply because we have to face anew the same dangers?" And the little pedagogue's eyes fairly beamed with patriotic ardor.

"I must confess that to do so would look like we had turned cowards after bravely winning only one-half the battle," answered Weston. "To desert the negro now and leave him to the mercy of the rebellious, liberty-hating and slavery-loving Bourbons, who have such an insane desire to keep him in ignorance, and consequent semi-slavery, that their most inveterate hatred is directed against those who seek to enlighten him, is to rob the poor negro of the real fruit of our victory in battle, and leave him with only the empty hull."

"That is the true sentiment, and fitly expressed," said Tinklepaugh.

"I have often wondered at the indifference manifested by our people up North in respect to the situation down South," said Weston, after a pause. "The North gave the negro his freedom, and afterwards clothed him with the emblematic weapon of a freeman, the ballot; and it does seem to me, that if the old proslavery element continues much longer to deprive him of his right to exercise his privilege as a citizen, and continues to kill and whip those who seek to instruct him how to perform the duties of citizenship, the general government ought to interfere and protect him in his rights—and his instructors, too—by direct governmental aid."

"I agree with you exactly in that," answered Tinklepaugh, "and I desire to speak with you further on that subject, and privately ; but let my students now give you a few readings and recitations, and I will then dismiss the school for the day."

"I will be delighted to hear them," answered Weston, wishing to cultivate as strong a friendship with the little teacher as possible, and well knowing that a manifestation of sympathy with him in his work was the most effective way of reaching him.

The school consisted of about forty dusky students, and was made up of nearly all ages. The little ragged and dirty urchin was there, with his little primer with big flaming letters ; the athletic youth and kinky-headed maiden, with their spelling-books and first readers ; the middle-aged man and matron, who sometimes exchanged for the purpose of reciting the well-thumbed and dirty little primer with their own offspring; and even the gray-haired son of slavery was there, who had wasted his strength, both mental and physical, before being accorded the privilege of atttending school—all of them exceedingly anxious to "git an eddication, an' be like de white folks."

They were all more or less embarrassed by the unexpected appearance and presence of their visitor, for few white people had ever had the temerity to visit that school; but their pieces were generally well delivered, and all acquitted themselves creditably, everything considered. A few of them read difficult selections very intelligently, and the delivery of some of the recitations evinced a considerable degree of talent in the reciter, though negroes always recite and declaim well if properly trained. Their voices are more musical than those of the Caucasian, and their intonation better, provided there be equal culture and preparation. One of the recitations, by a full-chested and deep-voiced young man of about twenty-five, was especially well rendered, and it is here reproduced in full, though with regret that it is impossible to reproduce on paper the perfect intonation of voice and admirable change from an expression of levity, in the opening verses, to one of deep-sorrow, toward the close, followed by an expression of hope, as set forth in the last two verses. The Negro is a natural imitator and mimicker, and the young man gave both voice and limbs full sway as he recited:

MY BRUDDER SAM AN' I.

De happiest niggers on de farm
   Was brudder Sam and I;
We never thought to do no harm,
   We nebber wouldn't try.

We had to work so hard all day,
   Ob which we was not fond;
But den, at twelve, we'd hab our play
   A swimmin' in de pond.

At night, before we went to res',
   My brudder Sam would sing,
An' I would pat, while Bob and Jess
   Went round and round de ring.

We danced de double-shuffle den;
  We made de welkin ring;
We made de kitchen trimble when
  We cut de " pijen·wing."

Ole massa, he'd step in de do',
  Or in de winder thrust
His silbry head to see de show,
  An' laff till he'd almos' bust.

Ole missus, she was funny, too,
  An' laffed wid ole Mars John;
An' often, when de play was through,
  Would ax another song.

But dat good time hab done and fled,
  'Twill nebber come no more;
For brudder Sam is done gone dead—
  Is gone to de oder shore.

My brudder Sam was black as tar,
  His eyes was big an' white;
He went wid massa to de war—
  He axed him if he might.

An' I remember well de hour
  Dat come for us to part;
His partin' words fell like a shower
  Ob snow upon my heart.

" Oh, brudder Sam, I lub you so——"
  'Tis thus I would begin;
But massa said I couldn't go,
  And den I cried agin.

We all did cry, an' cry, an' cry;
  'Tis sad to part, you know;
I thought ole missus sure would die,
  To see ole massa go.

" But we'll come back," ole massa said,
  " We'll come agin, some day,"
An' den he left us, an' he led
  My brudder Sam away.

I watched 'em passin' down de lane,
  Where many times we played;
Dey nebber passed dat way again—
  On de battle-field dey stayed.

One day dere came a letter back,
  Which missus quickly read;
She said de thing had gone to rack,
  An' brudder Sam was dead!

At las' de cruel war broke up,
  Dey hushed de battle roar;
But still dere's bitter in my cup,
  For brudder Sam's no more.

O'er field an' hill, an' on de shore,
  In sadness, still, I roam;
But brudder Sam I see no more—
  He nebber does come home.

His grave is on de Georgia plain,
  Oh, miles an' miles from here;
Dere falls de gentle summer rain,
  An' flowers am bloomin' near.

Some day de Lord will say to me,
  " Come up, come up, to home;
Come up, an' all my glories see,
  No more on earth you roam."

Oh, den I'll rise, on snowy wing,
  Up to de distant sky,
An' dere will join once more an' sing,
  My brudder Sam an' I.

At the conclusion of this recitation, Tinklepaugh tapped the school-bell, and the little black brats scrambled and tumbled over each other in their efforts to get out, just like white brats. As soon as the last little kinky head was out of sight, as they all went galloping, pell-mell, and screaming down the road, Weston turned to Tinklepaugh and said :

"I have sought this interview with you, Mr. Tinklepaugh, because I have been informed, by those who are supposed to know, that you are a man to be relied on when any service is to be performed for the benefit of the party; and I wish to confer with you in regard to the advisability of taking certain steps to insure a majority for our party at the approaching election. You are aware that the election comes off on the first Thursday in August, and, so far, very little effort has been made to put into operation all the election machinery at our disposal."

"I am very glad to hear you talk that way," answered Tinklepaugh. "Indeed, I have been very much mortified at the indifference and inactivity displayed by the leaders of our party so far. The powerful measures resorted to by the Ku-Klux Democrats to defeat us at the polls, in August, makes the situation somewhat alarming."

"And yet we can beat them easily, if we will only use all the means in our power properly," said Weston.

"Certainly we can," answered Tinklepaugh; "but how can we do anything so long as our Governor listens more to the voice of members of the Inter-States Land and Improvement Company than to the wail of Ku-

Klux victims? He has been importuned time and again to declare this county in a state of insurrection, and to call out the militia, under the wise provisions of the Ku-Klux bill; but members of the various land and improvement companies protest against such action, simply because they say it would prevent the influx of capital into the State for the Governor to declare officially that insurrection existed in the State. He must be interested in some of the companies himself."

"Perhaps a few more outrages would open his eyes," suggested Weston.

"But they don't occur," answered Tinklepaugh sorrowfully.

"Why can't we make them occur? What has become of the loyal Union League?"

"Oh, that organization belongs to the negroes, you know, and they are all natural cowards. The League at this place started out manfully to burn all the barns and granaries belonging to the Ku-Klux, in order to make the Klan retaliate by whipping and killing Republicans; but at the first crack of a pistol in the hands of a disguised Ku-Klux, they all faltered and hid, although they were acting, as they said, under the orders of the Governor himself, though I never believed that."

"My own election comes off at the general election in August," said Weston; "and unless I can have the aid of the presence of the military at the polls, I fear I shall be defeated. The negro is afraid to vote under the eyes of a Ku-Klux, and unless they have something to sustain them, they will refuse to vote."

"And even with the aid of troops at the polls we are not going to have a walk-over," answered Tinklepaugh.

"I have carefully considered the situation, and I tell you the odds are against us."

"I would rather die than to be defeated," said Weston, "and my opponent is not a man to be despised as an antagonist, but one rather to be dreaded."

"Colonel William Goldston is your opponent, I believe," said Tinklepaugh.

"Yes, and he is a shrewd debater, and is thoroughly conversant with the political history of the State, while my own knowledge in that particular is extremely meagre," answered Weston.

"Oh, well, never mind him," answered Tinklepaugh. "We'll treat him again as we did when he was elected to the Legislature in 1868."

"And how was that?" asked Weston.

"Why," he answered, "have you never heard about that? The Democrats bull-dozed enough voters to elect him to the Legislature in 1868, but when he got there he was compelled to stand aside, and was not permitted to take the oath of office."

"And how," asked Weston, "could they prevent him from taking the oath of office if he presented his certificate of election?"

"Oh, that was simple enough," answered Tinklepaugh. "You see he was sheriff of West county before the war, and under the provisions of the "Iron-Clad Oath," as the Democrats term it, no person who held office before the war, and afterwards engaged in the rebellion, is eligible to office now; and so, when he presented himself for installation into office, he was not permitted to be sworn in as a member of the Legislature. And twelve others were treated in the same way."

"I never heard of that before," said Weston. "In fact, I never before had any idea of the practical operation of that provision of the oath required by the act of Congress."

"You see we have everything in our own hands, if we will only use the means within our reach to perpetuate our power," answered Tinklepaugh.

"Yes, but with the indomitable and fearless Ku-Klux to fight, and a weak-kneed Governor sitting at the helm to direct our own war-ship, it appears to me that the enemy has the advantage of us after all," said Weston.

"But we must use our power," answered Tinklepaugh, with emphasis, "and I tell you there is but one way to prevent our defeat at the polls in August."

"And what is that?" asked Weston.

"For the Governor to order out the militia, and let them arrest and detain in prison, until after the election, enough Democrats to ensure a victory for us," answered Tinklepaugh.

"But how shall the Governor be induced to act?"

"Stir up such a scene of carnage and bloodshed that it will be his duty to do so, under the Ku-Klux act."

"But how can that be done? The negroes refuse to act, and shall we shed blood with our own hands?"

"Incite the members of the Union League to do it. It is not necessary for us to imbue our own hands in blood."

"But how?"

"By bribery. Money will buy a negro's soul."

"But where is the money to come from?"

"Out of the pockets of the slain."

For a few moments both villains sat and meditated in silence.   At last Weston spoke:

"And how would old Jasper Fontell do to begin with ?   He sold a gold mine to an English syndicate, a few weeks ago, and, besides, he has a stack of railroad bonds."

"He is the very man," answered Tinklepaugh. "His coffers are filled with gold and bonds, and we can empty his money-chests at the same time we drain his heart of its blood, and while we paint the bloody picture for the Governor with his gore, we can buy power with his gold."

"And influence with his bonds," said Weston.   "I tell you there is nothing like having a pile of railroad bonds to give one influence in the State.   With his bonds in our pockets, we may make ourselves stock-holders and directors in some of the new railroads."

"Pshaw!" answered Tinklepaugh, "these railroads will never be built.   It was never intended that they should be; but, then, the bonds are good, anyway, because they pledge the faith of the State, and ample provision will be made for their payment and redemption.   But how shall we proceed to procure those bonds? What precautions are necessary, in order that it may appear that he was certainly murdered by the Ku-Klux on account of his political opinions?"

"That is the point," answered Weston.   "It must certainly appear to be a political murder, and there must be sufficient evidence to implicate the Ku-Klux. I would never consent to the killing of any man, unless satisfied that his death would serve the interests of the party."

"Nor I, either," answered Tinklepaugh. "Fealty to the party, and a sincere desire to promote its interests, are the only motives that could prompt me to consent to his death, and it may be that we will serve the party in more ways than one by putting old Fontell out of the way. I am told that he is already weakening in his support of the party, and if we can kill a Democrat, and make it appear that the Ku-Klux have killed a Republican, we will deprive the Democrats of one vote, at least, and then if the Governor will act in the matter, as he ought, we may be able to get many more of them out of the way before the election, without the spilling of more blood."

"If he has severed his connection with the party, then it will do no good to kill him," said Weston. "I deplore the necessity of resorting to such extreme measures, anyway."

"Oh, you may quiet all fears on that score," answered Tinklepaugh. "I have no idea he has ever told anyone that he was going to desert the party, and the Ku-Klux still regard him as a very obnoxious Republican."

"But why, then, do you say that he is weakening in his support of the party?" asked Weston.

"Oh, simply because I went to him, as chairman of the Republican Executive Committee of this county, a few days ago, and asked him for money to bribe the members of the Union League and spur them up to more active service, and he refused to contribute anything, and you know when a Republican becomes so lukewarm as to refuse to donate for the benefit of the party, he is no longer to be implicitly trusted."

"Especially one who has his safe full of State bonds

that were almost given to him for the sake of his influence," answered Weston.

"Yes," answered Tinklepaugh, "and those bonds were given him with the expectation of receiving a large contribution from him to the campaign fund, and I reminded him of that fact the other day, but it seemed to do no good."

"Well," said Weston, "it seems to me that a man who has received the pecuniary favors bestowed by the party, and then refuses to aid us in time of need, ought to be gotten rid of, somehow, and I am more than ever satisfied that his early demise is a political necessity."

"Then I understand it is a settled fact that he must go," said Tinklepaugh.

"Yes," answered Weston.

"Then leave the details of the plot to me."

"Why?"

"Because," answered Tinklepaugh, "in the first place, it is impossible to make all the preliminary arrangements without first seeing the captain of the Union League, and finding out just how many will participate in the deed; and, besides, the woods are full of armed Ku-Klux, who are ever on the alert, and if we should be detected and captured it would never do for you to be along."

"And why not let me be caught as well as you?" asked Weston.

"Because you are the Solicitor for this judicial district," answered Tinklepaugh.

"And what has my official position to do with a midnight assassination, to which I would be, at least, an accessory before the fact?"

"Oh, a great deal," answered Tinklepaugh. "In the first place, if I should be arrested, you could use your official influence to have me released on straw bail, and I could then make my escape; but if you should be caught——well, we will not discuss that matter, since you will not be allowed to go."

"I see your point," answered Weston, admiring the ingenuity of his co-conspirator, "and I am willing to trust you to execute the scheme in every particular. But where shall we meet after the work is accomplished?"

"To divide the spoils, you mean?" asked Tinklepaugh.

"Yes."

"In your room at your hotel."

"But why not let me come to you? You seem to take all the work upon yourself."

"I tell you it will never do for you to be at all active in the matter," answered Tinklepaugh emphatically. "If our scheme succeeds and the Governor declares this county in a state of insurrection, there will be mutiny sure enough, and a reign of terror in the community, and every movement of yours will be watched on account of your official position."

"Very well," answered Weston; "I see I can rely on your judgment. But when shall the work be done, and when shall the meeting take place?"

"The work shall be done immediately, and the meeting will take place on the night afterwards," answered Tinklepaugh.

"At the Midland hotel?"

"At the Midland hotel in Westville. I know the place," answered Tinklepaugh.

"Can you obtain real Ku-Klux disguises for our men?". asked Weston.

"We have them already prepared," answered Tinklepaugh, "and have used them on a number of occasions."

"And the Ku-Klux have been saddled with the crimes committed," said Weston. "May you succeed in this instance as well."

"Trust me to carry the plot to a successful execution," answered Tinklepaugh, "and reserve all your power and ingenuity for what might happen hereafter."

"Good; I can trust you," answered Weston, rising from his seat on the steps of the rude hut to take his leave.

"Wait one moment," said Tinklepaugh, seeing Weston about to bid him good-bye. "There is another matter, I wish to speak to you about, and one that concerns, us both if we wish to see our schemes succeed."

"And what is that?" asked Weston, curious to know what further the sagacious little pedagogue had to suggest.

"Why, we will need a newspaper," answered Tinklepaugh.

"And what do we want with a newspaper, I should like to know?" said Weston. "Do you expect to kill old Fontell with vituperation and abuse published in a newspaper? I had anticipated that you would resort to more violent measures."

"And so we will, in his case," answered Tinklepaugh; "but that is only the beginning of the execution of our scheme, you know, and if we wish to carry it out to the fullest extent, we must inflame the public mind with stories of Ku-Klux outrages until it will make the blood curdle in one's veins to hear them, and there is no other means so effectual to stir up the public mind to mutiny and rage as a newspaper published on the scene of disturbance, and edited by some one who is capable of depicting the horrors of sedition in the blackest colors."

"The newspaper, then, is to work upon the minds of the Governor and the leaders of the party," said Weston.

"Yes," answered Tinklepaugh, "that is the scheme."

"And a capital scheme it is, too," answered Weston; "a capital one, indeed. I am surprised that we had not thought of that before. But who can we get to edit such a paper?"

"The first question is, where can we get the money to purchase the outfit?" answered Tinklepaugh.

"Oh, we can find the money very easily," said Weston. "I will furnish the money myself, if no one else can be found willing to advance it, simply for the benefit I hope it will be to me in the election."

"Then, if you furnish the money, you will be sole owner of the paper, and might nominate the editor yourself," answered Tinklepaugh.

"Then I nominate you," said Weston. "Will you accept?"

"Let me see," said Tinklepaugh, pretending to hesitate and reflect a moment; "Yes; my school will be out tomorrow, and I will accept the position at once."

"Very well," answered Weston, "I will have posters to announce the appearance of the paper on next

8

Wednesday morning. But what shall we name the infant?"

"Oh, anything you suggest," answered Tinklepaugh.

"Then we will call it the *Westville Republican*," said Weston.

"I presume you wish it to be a rival of the *Westville Conservative*, edited by Albert Seaton," said Tinkle-paugh.

"Yes, and a terror to all such Ku-Klux politicians," answered Weston. "But what night shall I expect you to attend to old man Fontell?"

"On next Saturday night," answered Tinklepaugh, "and I will have a full account of the affair in the first edition of the *Westville Republican*."

"And a true account," laughed Weston, as he entered his carriage and bade Tinklepaugh good-bye a second time.

"Yes, a true account, as we would wish the Governor to see it," laughed Tinklepaugh in reply, as the wheels of the carriage commenced to rattle on the road toward Westville.

"By Jove! I am glad I met him," said Tinklepaugh to himself, as the top of the carriage disappeared in the distance. "I have been wanting some person of his ilk to co-operate with me for some time, and he seems to be the very character I have been looking for. And when I get to be editor of that paper, every article shall be written with a pen dipped in gall, and the hand that guides the pen shall be propelled by malignity, hate, rancor and malice, until the very streets of Westville shall be red with the blood of those who have sneered and scoffed at me on account of my present occupation.

CHAPTER IX.

A KU-KLUX OUTRAGE.

Mr. Jasper Fontell, commonly known in the community as "Old Stingy Jap," lived in a very large and commodious, but somewhat dilapidated, house about a mile from Westville. He had succeeded in worrying his wife to death, by his penurious habits, many years before the events recorded in this book occurred, and had placed her away in the little family burying ground back of the garden, with a decaying piece of rude plank at the head of her grave, on which he carved (with his own hand to avoid having any expense attached to the funeral) the simple letters "M. F.", which those who knew her before her decease interpreted to mean "Mary Fontell"; but, except for the humble grave and the two simple letters on the rough board at the head of it, there was nothing in or about the house to indicate that such a person had ever lived there. They never had any children, and "Stingy Jap" now lived all alone with no one to quarrel at, save a big bull-dog by the name of "Towser."

No opprobrious sobriquet was ever more appropriately and deservedly bestowed on any human being than that of "Stingy Jap", as applied to old Jasper Fontell, as Towser himself testified a thousand times—indeed, at every meal-time; and Towser had been the old man's solitary companion ever since "M. F." perished in body, mind and soul, and found relief in the lowly grave in rear of the garden, where she was placed by her surviving consort with no more manifestation of love or sympathy than she had enjoyed during her long and miserable connubial existence. Old Fontell was, in fact, a miser in every sense of that term, save in one particular : a real miser generally converts everything around him into money, and hoards it in secret niches in the wall of the house, or buries it in the ground ; whereas, "Stingy Jap" invested his earning in stocks, bonds and real estate, and in all his bargains he exhibited a shrewdness that showed him to be a financier of no mean ability. And yet, he loved to sit and count his money just like every other miser, and often after selling a valuable piece of property, for his rule was always to sell at the first advance in the price, he would sit and rattle his gold-bag at Towser, and Towser would growl at him in reply, and accuse him of being too stingy to give his dog bread enough to eat. He shut himself out from all society, and paid little attention to the affairs of church or State, consequently he received no visitors, and had no communication with any person except on matters of business. It might be expected that such a character would have few friends and sympathizers, and

> "Alas, for the rarity
> Of human charity
> Under the sun,

it must be recorded of him that his friends were, indeed, few. And yet he had one friend, a near neighbor, who sometimes paid the old man a visit, notwithstanding his repulsive demeanor toward his visitors and evident dislike for them.

This good neighbor, Mr. Garrett Dixon, was enjoying the pleasant shade on his front piazza, and inhaling the fragrant odors that came from the profusion of flowers in the yard, on the morning of the second Sunday in June, 1870, when his wife came out and handed him a little basket filled with pretty red June apples.

"I thought you would enjoy a few of them this morning," she said. "They are so early and nice, too. Nobody in the neighborhood has any like them."

"Thank you," said Mr. Dixon, politely, for a man never ceases to be polite to his wife as long as he loves her; "they are very nice, indeed. Have one, too."

"No," said his wife, "I have just eaten a few in the orchard while gathering them, and I don't care for any more."

"But I don't like to enjoy such luxuries by myself," said Mr. Dixon, good naturedly. "It seems to me, I ought to divide with somebody."

"I'll tell you whom you can divide with," said his wife, "and it will be an act of real charity, too."

"Who?"

"Old Stingy Jap."

"True, I had not thought of him," said Mr. Dixon. "And it *will* be an act of charity to divide with him, as you suggest, for I doubt if there is an apple or a peach on his plantation, though he is well able to afford Malaga grapes as a luxury, if he was not too stingy."

"Well, we are not responsible for his penuriousness, and it seems that he can't help it himself," answered Mrs. Dixon.

"That is true," said Mr. Dixon, "and I hope I can give him the apples with as much real pleasure as it would afford me to give a piece of bread to a starving beggar. He is certainly poor in one respect, notwithstanding his gold, and his bonds, and his lands: he certainly suffers the poverty of human sympathy, which is the worst form of poverty after all, and if it be said that he shuns and repulses those around him, it must be admitted in reply that the world has neglected and repulsed him, too."

"I will call a servant to take them over for you," said Mrs. Dixon.

"No," answered Mr. Dixon, "it is not very far, and the sun is not up enough to be hot yet, and so I prefer to take them myself."

Mr. Dixon took the basket on his arm, and proceeded over to his neighbor's house by a little path that led through the woods, which was shady and pleasant. The path led up to a little yard gate, on the back side of the house, and Mr. Dixon entered this quietly, for fear of arousing Towser, and walked around the house to the front door. But he did not knock—he started to, but his arm was arrested at the sight of a most hideous picture on the door, and he stood for a few moments transfixed to the spot, trembling with fright and astonishment. On the door was a picture of a skull and cross-bones, a coffin and a scythe blade, and under these figures, evidently written in human blood, were the portentous letters, "K. K. K."

Recovering his self-possession, after a few moments, Mr. Dixon turned to leave, when his eyes encountered a sight more appalling still. Suspended to a limb of a tree in the yard, was the lifeless form of old Jasper Fontell! The body was cold and rigid; his eye-balls had bursted from their sockets; one hand was partly uplifted, as if in supplication, and everything around gave evidence of the most violent contortions in death. The knot in the rope had been clumsily tied, and had slipped around to one side of his neck, pressing his head forward and toward the opposite side; his mouth was wide open, and his black, swollen tongue was resting on his shoulder. He presented a frightful spectacle, indeed, and Mr. Dixon did not linger long to see it. Towser was still there, sitting a few paces off, and looking up into the face of his dead master with an expression of genuine pity; but the voice of the poor dog was dumb as to the identity of the perpetrators of the horrible deed, and he could only express his sympathy and affection for the deceased by a low and pitiful whine. Mr. Dixon tried for a few moments to coax Towser home with him, for the purpose of feeding the poor brute, but no amount of persuasion could induce him to desert the form of his lifeless master.

Hurrying home, Mr. Dixon informed his wife of the horrible discovery, and then hastily left to summon his neighbors and acquaint them with the facts. A messenger was immediately dispatched to Westville for the county coroner, and very soon that important functionary appeared and summoned a jury to inquire into the cause of the death. The jury having been sworn and empannelled, in proper form of law, the next thing necessary was to secure witnesses, and quite a number were sworn and examined, without eliciting anything of importance. The coroner was about to adjourn the inquest with the usual verdict of a coroner's jury— "that the deceased came to his death by violence at the hands of some person or persons unknown"—when some one suggested that it would be proper to send for the district Solicitor, and have the benefit of his advice and assistance in the investigation. It was unanimously agreed that this was the proper thing to do, under the circumstances, and so another messenger was hastily despatched for Donald Weston, Esq., the district Solicitor.

The person making this suggestion might have explained to the crowd that he had been directed by Mr. Weston to demand his attendance and official assistance at the proper time, but that information belonged exclusively to the elect, the inner circle, and the vulgar, common mind had no business knowing such things. Weston soon appeared, clothed in his official power and dignity, and surveyed the premises with a well-feigned shudder of horror. "I see, gentlemen," said that dignitary, averting his eyes from the ghastly form of the dead man swinging in the air before him, and pointing to the ominous representation on the door, "that there is some evidence that the unfortunate deceased met his death by violence committed by a secret, lawless organization. We all know the meaning and origin of those menacing warnings on the door yonder, and we all know, too, the dangers incurred by witnesses who possess the bravery to testify against the perpetrators of such deeds, and I therefore advise and direct that this inquest be held in secret."

The coroner at once concurred in this view of the case, and approved the direction given by the Solicitor to hold a secret inquest. Accordingly, the jury, all of whom had been selected with care from those who were known to be ardent Republicans, were directed to retire to an old woodshed in one corner of the yard, and no one was thereafter allowed to approach within hearing distance, except the witnesses as they were examined.

What was said and done by this secret, partisan inquisition after their retirement, can only be guessed at from what transpired after their adjournment, and these things will be fully detailed in subsequent chapters.

CHAPTER X.

THE TWO VILLAINS MEET AGAIN.

"Fo' de Lawd, Mr. Tinkerpy," said Uncle Ben as he conducted the future editor of the Westville *Republican* up stairs to Weston's room, at the Midland hotel, on Sunday evening, "I had no idee ob seein' you in town to-night. Glad to see ye, do'. 'Deed, I'se allus glad to see enny white man, what teaches de cullud folks an edicashun like de white folks,"

"Much obliged to you for your kind appreciation of my work, in trying to improve the condition of your race," answered Tinklepaugh; "and I am happy to be able to inform you that I am henceforth to serve your slavery-cursed and oppressed people in an enlarged capacity."

"What yer mean, Mr. Tinkerpy," said Uncle Ben, half comprehending Tinklepaugh's meaning, "sho' yer aint er gwine ter quit yer school?"

"Yes, Uncle Ben," answered Tinklepaugh, "I have abandoned that avocation for the present."

"De Lawd hab mercy on de po' niggers!" exclaimed Uncle Ben. "An' ye's done gone an' 'zerted us too, Mr. Tinkerpy. Fo' God, it seems de niggers hab no fren's no mo', an' dey gwine ter be 'lowed ter die in dere ig'nance, jes' like in slabery times."

"Why, Uncle Ben," answered Tinklepaugh, "you must have misunderstood me, when I told you I was now prepared to serve you more efficiently than ever before. I am going to be the editor of a newspaper that is to be devoted exclusively to the amelioration of the condition of your race, both politically and socially."

"A newspaper," exclaimed Uncle Ben, "an' what's ter become ob de school?"

"Oh, I do not know what will become of it, for the present," answered Tinklepaugh. "My time expired, and I was offered a position in an enlarged sphere of usefulness, both to the colored race and to the Republican party, and I felt it to be my duty to accept. At present there is no newspaper in this section of the State that devotes even a column to the interests of the colored people, and I think they ought to have some such medium of communication with the world."

"But what good will de paper do when de po' nigger kaint read it?" asked Uncle Ben deprecatingly.

"Well, Uncle Ben," answered Tinklepaugh, somewhat stunned at the point so suddenly suggested, "it does seem that your people ought to be prepared to read and enjoy what is written and published for your special benefit; but, then, you have other interests that ought to be dearer to you than a knowledge of books. The preservation of your liberties and rights as citizens is a matter of more importance to you just now than the acquisition of knowledge, and I propose that my paper shall be an exponent of your higher interests."

"Den, is de Democrat party gwine ter take de nigger's freedom erway from him, sho' nuff?" asked Uncle Ben.

"They will, if they ever once acquire the power," answered Tinklepaugh. "I tell you the political ascendency of that party would mean the destruction of the liberties of your people."

"Dat's what be jedge an' Mister Weston bof tells me," said Uncle Ben, "an' I begins to belebe it, too, do' I did say I'd nebber vote de 'Publican ticket no mo', unless dey gib us de forty acres an' de mule, like dey promised us 'fo de las' 'lection."

"Well, Uncle Ben, you must not be in too great a hurry," answered Tinklepaugh. "You must remember it takes time to accomplish great undertakings."

"It's bin three years," answered Uncle Ben, whose heart was set on the acquisition of the promised bounty, "an' I haint seed a single nigger wid de forty acres an' de mule, an' it 'pears ter me dey hab had time er plenty ter make er beginnin'."

"Well, we have had so many other important things to attend to that we have hardly had time to consider that matter," said Tinklepaugh. "But the party has done what was best for your interests, you may be assured. What good would it do you to own the forty acres and the mule, when the bare possession of them would make you the object of Ku-Klux enmity, and might possibly result in your becoming their victim? Don't you know they whip and kill every colored man who, even by his own labor and economy, acquire a little property?"

"Well, I'se heered dat dey do," answered Uncle Ben, still clinging to the idea that the negroes had been cheated, "but if dey would gib me de forty acres an' de mule, I'd resk de chuck-a-lucks."

But Uncle Ben's discussion of his favorite theme was suddenly terminated by the appearance of Weston, and, picking up his hat, he reluctantly left the room, muttering to himself as he descended the stairway that "de 'Publican party done fooled us once er bout de forty acres an' de mule."

"You must excuse my want of punctuality in keeping my appointment," said Weston to Tinklepaugh, as he cordially grasped the hand of the ex-teacher. "I was somewhat belated by the prolonged investigation before the coroner's inquest, and reached home only a few moments ago."

"I have been very comfortable here since my arrival," answered Tinklepaugh, "and have been somewhat entertained, as well as amused, by the conversation of your servant. He seems to be very much aggrieved because he has never received the forty acres and the mule we promised them. Really, I am afraid he will desert the party on that account."

"Yes," answered Weston, "that old Ku-Klux chieftain, Major Wyland, has filled his head with that notion, and his mind is only capable of holding one idea at a time."

"Perhaps a little discipline would do him good," suggested Tinklepaugh.

"From whom?"

"From the Union League. Have you not heard of our latest order?"

"No," answered Weston; "what is it?"

"Why, to whip every negro who does not promise to vote the Republican ticket at the approaching election," answered Tinklepaugh. "It is said the order emanates from the Governor, who is recognized as the head of the League in this State."

"But how is the negro to know that he is not being whipped by the Ku-Klux because of his affiliation with the Republican party, instead of by the League, on account of his desertion of the party?"

"Oh, we inform him of the cause of his punishment at the time it is inflicted," answered Tinklepaugh. "But generally it is not necessary to resort to violence at all, for his promise is easily exacted upon the slightest demonstration of force."

"Yes, the negro will promise anything," answered Weston, "but the trouble is that in case you bribe him, he refuses to remain bribed, and may be purchased by the next man who meets him; and if you exact a promise from him by violence, or a threat of violence, he forgets it as soon as the force is removed, and the next man who lifts a whip over his head can make him break his contract by promising to do the very opposite."

"Well, it does seem that he is naturally a perverse being, anyway," said Tinklepaugh, "and it is only a question of who gets him last. But a discussion of the negro problem is not our business to-night. We have more practical matters to attend to. Lock your room door."

While Weston was complying with this precautionary injunction, Tinklepaugh unlocked a medium sized valise which he had brought with him, and emptied its contents on the table before him.

"And now for a division of the spoils," said Tinklepaugh, with a wicked grin, as Weston took a seat on the opposite side of the table. "Here is our legacy under the will of 'Old Stingy Jap.'"

"It is not by virtue of his *will*, I dare say," answered Weston. "Not, indeed, unless his mind underwent a considerable change *in articulo mortis*, and you induced him to bequeath the legacy through undue influence."

"Well," answered Tinklepaugh, with a wicked leer, "I must confess, that those who ministered to his wants in his last moments would be compelled to testify that his 'ruling passion was strong in death'; but still he left his property behind him, and, as he left no children to inherit it, we took it as a gift *causa mortis*."

"And a princely bequest it is, too," said Weston.

"Yes, and as a token of our appreciation of the princely gift, we swung him up in regal style," answered Tinklepaugh.

"I thought it was rather a bungling job, as I viewed it," answered Weston. "The knot in the rope had slipped around to one side of his neck, which turned his head so that he seemed to be trying to look back at something behind him."

"Oh, that was his greedy eyes trying to follow us, I reckon, as we made off with the booty," answered Tinklepaugh.

"Well, it would seem that his voracious eyes did try to follow you," answered Weston. "They had actually crawled out of their sockets in pursuit of you."

"Well, for fear he should really come back and claim the plunder, let's divide it and appropriate it to our own use while we possess it," answered Tinklepaugh.

"Good!" answered Weston; "reach me those bonds, and let me count them."

The bonds were counted and found to foot up forty thousand dollars.

"Forty thousand!" ejaculated Weston. "A royal gift, indeed. How shall we divide them?"

"Equally, of course," answered Tinklepaugh. "One suggested and planned, and the other executed. An equal division is equitable."

"That is twenty thousand each," said Weston, eyeing the bonds with the cupidity of a Jew. "And how much is there of the gold?"

"Count it," answered Tinklepaugh.

"Ten thousand," said Weston after he had arranged it, in stacks of one hundred dollars each, on the table.

"Yes," answered Tinklepaugh; "there were a few hundred dollars over, but I had to divide that among the band of black mercenaries, who relieved old Fontell while I hunted up the skids."

"You were very liberal with them," suggested Weston. "I wonder that they would consent to receive so small a share out of so large a pile."

"As to the amount," answered Tinklepaugh, "they had no idea of that, for I kept the whole thing carefully concealed, and left them under the impression that I had made an equal division with them. And as for my liberality, my only fear is that I have been too liberal."

"And why so?"

"Why," answered Tinklepaugh, "you know it would never do for a negro to have a large sum of money about him. The fool couldn't keep it, if it represented his soul's salvation, and to spend it would create suspicion."

"I admire your shrewdness," answered Weston, "as

well as your disposition to take care of number one."

"And number *two*," suggested Tinklepaugh, pointing to Weston.

"Yes, and ' number two,' answered Weston. "I suppose I am 'number two' in this game, and your division with me has been made with the magnanimity of a prince."

" I was indebted to you, though, for the suggestion of Old Stingy Jap's name. I had long desired to stir up the public mind with some blood-curdling spectacle, but I had never thought of filling my empty pockets at the same time. Why, if it had not been for the hint received from you, I might have swooped down upon some beggar Republican, and got nothing for my pains. Nobody like a lawyer for killing two birds with one stone."

" Well, we will not discuss our relative merits in the transaction," said Weston ; "for business of more importance demands our attention. We have accomplished only half our object, you know."

" Yes, and this money must be devoted to the furtherance of our schemes and the benefit of the party," answered Tinklepaugh.

"And the bonds for our own pleasure and individual promotion," said Weston, as he imitated his crafty friend by carefully placing the bonds in the bottom of a little box (which Tinklepaugh had taken the precaution to provide) and piled the gold on top of them.

"Why, your heart seems to be as much set on the bonds as Uncle Ben's is on the forty acres and the mule!" laughed Tinklepaugh.

9

"With this difference," answered Weston, with an avaricious smile: "that I have acquired, in a reasonable measure, the object of my desire, while Uncle Ben will never realize any portion of his."

"Poor credulous darkies!" said Tinklepaugh, feigning a sympathy he never really felt; "they can be gulled into doing almost anything; and, yet, I fear that a good many of them are beginning to lose faith in the promises of 1868, like Uncle Ben, and that we will have to invent some new scheme to preserve the full strength of that race for our party in the coming election."

"Keep telling them that the Democrats will reduce them to slavery again, if they obtain control of the government," answered Weston. "The negro is naturally timid, and the idea is to play upon his fears. I tell you if we will only play that racket properly, there is not one of them that will ever vote the Democratic ticket, so long as a living one of them can show the marks of the lash on his back. It beats the cry of the forty acres and the mule all to pieces."

"That is the idea I have been insisting upon for some time," answered Tinklepaugh, "and I shall adopt that policy in the *Westville Republican.*"

"No, I doubt the wisdom of proclaiming any such absurdity in public print," answered Weston. "Every body who has intelligence enough to read a newspaper knows that slavery is dead, and will have sense enough to see that the issue is kept alive solely for partisan purposes, and I think it would be bad policy to charge, publicly, that the Democrats would reduce the negro to slavery if raised to political power. Let that he done secretly, in Union Leagues and at their churches and school-houses."

"Ah, I see your ideas are correct, and that I shall need your counsel in shaping the policy of the paper," answered Tinklepaugh. "But what about the mechanical part of the work and the press and fixtures? Have these things been provided?"

"Everything is in readiness, as I promised you it should be," answered Weston. "I ordered a press and outfit immediately after leaving you, the other day, and received a letter yesterday evening, saying they would surely reach here to-morrow morning, and two competent printers have already arrived from Washington."

"Then I must proceed at once with the preparation of the subject-matter of the first issue," said Tinklepaugh.

"Yes," answered Weston, "but, first, we must prepare and send off a telegram to Northern daily journals, giving an account of the latest and most horrible Ku-Klux outrage."

"Another good idea!" said Tinklepaugh. "Let those great metropolitan journals horrify the public mind with daily accounts of the frightful scene, and the *Westville Republican*, next Wednesday, will confirm the story by giving all the ghastly details."

So the two villains concocted and telegraphed the following frightful story, which appeared next morning in all the great newspapers of the day, in this form:

"KU–KLUXISM!

"Murder Most Foul!

"*A Reign of Terror in the South!*

"Last night at midnight there was committed, in West county, one of the most horrible murders ever known in the annals of crime. A band of over five hundred murderous Ku-Klux, disguised and armed to the teeth, rode boldly through the streets of the town of West-ville, just as the town clock was striking the hour of twelve, and proceeded to the home of Mr. Jasper Fon-tell, an aged and respectable citizen of the county, who lived only one mile from town, and there they hung, to a limb of a tree in the yard, this aged and venerable citizen until he was dead. Mr. Fontell was a wealthy and influential citizen, and lived alone in a magnificent mansion, near the public road leading out from the town of Westville, his beloved wife having died several years ago, leaving no children. He was quiet and un-obtrusive in his habits, and charitable almost to a fault; indeed, his home was a veritable alms-house, from which the needy and oppressed were never turned away com-fortless. His sympathies, notwithstanding his great wealth and high social position, were ever with the lowly and humble; and, indeed, the whole record of his life leaves no other conjecture as to the cause of his death but that he had incurred the enmity of the Ku-Klux, because he persisted in voting the Republican ticket. Heretofore, the victims of Ku-Klux outrages have been the weak, the ignorant and the helpless; but, in this instance, they have selected as their victim a man who was conspicuous for his possession and exercise of all the virtues that contribute to make true manhood, and his violent death shows only too plainly the inveterate malignity of the Ku-Klux toward all those, of whatever caste, who vote the Republican ticket. Mr. Fontell was certainly murdered for his political opinions. No other cause is assigned for the dastardly deed; no one has attempted to assign any other. The Ku-Klux, themselves, boast of their crime, and swear vengeance against all Republicans, white and black.

"How long, O Lord! how long, shall organized law-lessness stalk through the land unmolested and unopposed? How many more victims must be offered up, as martyrs to the cause of liberty and good government, before the ear of this great Republic will listen to the wail of distress? How much longer will the Governor of that great State sit idle in the executive chair and see the good citizens of his State, whom he has sworn to protect, butchered like dogs, and hung like felons, while the perpetrators of such deeds escape unpunished, and defy his authority?

"There is in the South, to-day, especially in certain districts, a reign of terror unequalled by anything connected with the French Revolution. Citizens are arming themselves, but they are powerless to cope with the members of a secret organization, who take good men out of their beds and hang them in front of their own doors, simply because they are suspected of being in sympathy with the Republican party; and still the government looks complacently on, and not a finger is lifted to stay the hand of violence. How long shall these things continue?"

CHAPTER XI.

INSURRECTION.

The "Battle of Bullets" ceased with the downfall of the Southern Confederacy in 1865 ; the "Battle of Ballots" began with the political ascendency of the negro, when he first exercised his right of suffrage, in 1867. Only two short years elapsed, from the time the manacles of slavery were finally shaken from the negro's ankles, until he stood before the world the proud possessor of all the dignity and insignia of rank enjoyed by sovereign citizens under the grandest republican government the world ever knew—until he stood, side by side, with his late master, his equal in every respect under the law. No such political metamorphosis of an enslaved race had ever occurred before in the history of the world; and statesmen, who remembered the lessons of history, beginning with the lesson taught by the compulsory sojourn of the Israelites in the wilderness for forty years, in order to prepare them for the duties of citizenship, looked on with horror and prophesied disaster. The radical reconstructionists of the North declared it to be the duty of the general government to protect the emancipated slaves—either by direct governmental interference, or, by enabling them to protect themselves, by giving them the means of local self-government; and with this plea, they attempted to justify their haste in clothing the negro with the ballot; while, on the other hand, those who knew the negro best, and feared his incapacity for self-government, became alarmed at the situation, and declared that Congress had made a mistake—that it ought to have waited until the negro should demonstrate his fitness for citizenship. It must be remembered, too, that the same act of Congress which gave the negro the ballot, deprived, by its unjust and iniquitous provisions, many thousands of white citizens of their elective franchise.

The prophecy of Southern statesmen was soon verified — negro voters became nothing more than tools in the hands of unprincipled politicians, who used them for their own self-aggrandisement. It has been said that a ballot falls—

> "As snow-flakes fall upon the sod;
> But executes a freeman's will
> As lightning does the will of God."

But ballots deposited by negro voters simply executed the will of the political satraps and adventurers, who directed them how to vote, and the voters themselves, in many instances, never even knew for whom or what they voted. A swarm of unprincipled carpet-baggers and scalawags took possession of Southern State governments, and the storm-swept and blood-drenched South became a platform of unbridled speculation and a pasture land for unprincipled greed, and the halls of the Legislatures dens of thieves. With one hand, they pointed to the black pictures and horrifying recitals of the wrongs and outrages, alleged to have been committed by the Ku-Klux, and, with the other, they reached deep down into the treasuries of the different States

and took out and squandered hundreds of thousands
of dollars of the people's money.   Honest men wrung
their hands in anguish, and cried out in despair:

> "A Roman sworder and banditte slaves
>   Murdered sweet Tully ; Brutus' bastard hand
>   Stabbed Julius Cæsar ; savage islanders
>   Pompey the Great ; and Suffolk dies by pirates."

Ku-Kluxism became a distaff and wheel upon which
resident demagogues of the carpet-bagger stripe spun
an endless thread of falsehood, and the warp and woof
thus furnished were woven into a cloth by Northern
newspapers that was used to cover and hide many of
the political sins of reconstruction.

Of all those who turned the wheel and spun the
threads of misrepresentation, which were woven into a
web of lies by these Northern outrage looms, none
worked more assiduously or effectively than the two
murderers of "Old Stingy Jap." The story of that crime
as telegraphed by these two little villains, and embel-
lished by the imagination of the weavers at the aforesaid looms, sent a thrill of terror throughout the country, and so startled the Governor that he instantly proclaimed West county to be in a state of insurrection.
Martial law was established in the county, and a company of mixed troops, under the immediate command
of Captain Crawford Tellefson, was stationed at Westville.

Captain Tellefson was a tall, gawky, clownish, lout-
ish scoundrel, against whom the Almighty had warned
the people by creating him cross-eyed, and as his name

was a little difficult to pronounce by the ignorant troops under his command, these motley ragamuffins had dubbed him "Cross-eyed Telf," a name which soon become a terror to every good citizen in West county.

Cross-eyed Telf soon formed an intimate acquaintance with Weston and Tinklepaugh, whom he regarded as the oracles of all wisdom, and these little scoundrels, finding a congenial spirit in Cross-eyed Telf, cultivated him for all he was worth, and made him the instrument by which many of their most wicked schemes were accomplished.

He established his quarters in the court-house, and converted all the offices in that temple of justice into barracks for his mercenaries, and the main court-room into a prison for his victims. The room usually occupied by the grand jury was reserved for a wine-room, in which was kept, not wine in fact, but the meanest kind of that distilled hell-broth, commonly known in the western counties as "moonshine," which meant (this explanation is for the benefit of the unsophisticated) whiskey that had escaped the vigilance of those revenue officers, properly designated as Deputy Marshals; but known, in mountain nomenclature, as "bung-smellers."

The first duty Cross-eyed Telf felt it incumbent upon him to perform, was to ferret out and have punished, the murderers of Old Stingy Jap, who had been proclaimed to the world as a martyr to the cause of liberty, and had been cononized as a political saint; and in this, as in all other things, he received the assistance and counsel of the district Solicitor, whose official duty it was to prosecute all offenders.

"This is a case, Captain Tellefson, that, so far, has

baffled my skill, both as a detective and as a lawyer,"
said Weston, a few mornings after the arrival of the
troops, to Cross-eyed Telf, who had come to consult one
of the oracles. "Immediately upon receiving the first
news of the terrible tragedy, I hastened to the scene of
the murder, and took the precaution to hold a secret
inquest before the coroner; but no facts were developed,
except that the crime was committed by armed Ku-
Klux in disguise."

"And who were the witnesses that testified to even
these few isolated facts?" asked Cross-eyed Telf, looking abstractedly out of the window of Weston's office, as
he (Weston) thought, but in reality directly at Weston.

"Oh, there were quite a number of them," answered
Weston, "and even those who were ardent Democrats
admitted that the men wore genuine Ku-Klux disguises. None of the witnesses actually saw the murder committed, for they were afraid to follow the band
of assassins, but they saw them on the road to and
from the house of Mr. Fontell."

"And did none of them observe any peculiarities of
size or form, by which some of the murderers could be
identified?" asked Crossed-eyed Telf.

"None of them," answered Weston.

"Then, it seems to me, that the clue is a very slight
one," said Cross-eyed Telf."

"Very slight, indeed," answered Weston. "We have
only the two segregate facts that the crime was committed by the Ku-Klux, and that there is a den of them
in the community known as Klan No. 40."

"And do you not know the members of that den?"
asked Cross-eyed Telf, again looking straight at Wes-

ton; but, as that worthy thought, directly out of the window.

"Yes, and that is another item I had forgotten," answered Weston.

"Aha! and an important one, too," answered Cross-eyed Telf, with a malicious wink, which Weston failed to observe, thinking he was still looking out of the window. "We have, then, three important facts established : First, that the crime was committed by the Ku-Klux ; second, there is a den of these cut-throats in the community ; and third, the names of the members of this den are known. It seems to me there is sufficient evidence to justify arrests."

"But whom shall we arrest ?" asked Weston. "There are more than a hundred members of the den, I am told, and the highest number on the raid at Fontell's, as testified to by the witnesses, was placed at forty, and we have no evidence to implicate any particular ones as constituting the forty."

"Oh, we are not in your civil courts just now," answered Cross-eyed Telf. "In your civil courts, you must have an investigation before a grand jury, and the charge in the presentment must be there sustained by proof, and then follows, I believe, a bill of indictment, and upon that a capias issues for the arrest of the offender ; but martial law is not encumbered and hampered by so much red tape. But your civil courts have played out, now, and my orders constitute the law in this county."

"What, then, do you propose to do ?" asked Weston.

"Why, I propose to arrest some of the most timid

of the members of the Klan, and extort a confession from them," answered Cross-eyed Telf.

"A good idea," said Weston. "You see I am rather green in military tactics. The idea of wrenching a confession out of them by torture, had not occurred to me."

"Give me the names of some of the members," said Cross-eyed Telf, "and I will attend to them to-night."

Weston took out of his pocket a list of the members of the Klan, which had been secured by Tinklepaugh, and handed it to Cross-eyed Telf. The truth is, that he and Tinklepaugh had already planned to have these arrests made, in case the county should be placed under military authority; and Tinklepaugh had already suggested the plan to Cross-eyed Telf, but Weston pretended to have learned it from Tellefson. The list included, among others, the names of Major Wyland, Albert Seaton, Samuel Washburn, John Latham and Henry Worthel, whom the reader already knows.

No sooner had the curtains of night spread themselves over the horror-stricken town, admonishing those who were weary with the toils and excitements of the day that it was time to retire to rest, than a squad of five mercenaries were detailed by Cross-eyed Telf to go to the house of John Latham, and arrest him and bring him before that military satrap. The heavy tread of Dick Madison, the big negro preacher and crier in Judge Farwell's court, aroused every inmate of the house, by the time he had crossed the front piazza and reached the door, and it is needless to add that Mrs. Latham was very much frightened by the appearance of so many persons, as the noise they made indicated, at such an unseasonable hour.

"Who is there?" asked John Latham, in answer to the knock with the ponderous fist of the burly preacher.

"Some sojers, wid a message from Capting Telf," answered the stentorian voice of the negro preacher.

"And what do you want?"

"We want yo' to come an' go wid us to see de Capting," answered Dick.

"And what business has he sending for folks at this unusual hour?" asked John. "Why couldn't he attend to such matters in the day time?"

"I dunno dat," answered Dick. "He jes' said fer us to fetch ye along, an' I guess yer better come wid us."

"Surely, you do not mean to arrest me and take me, whether I choose to go or not," said John, beginning to think seriously of the situation.

"Dem's de words he said," answered Dick, "to arrest ye, and fetch ye anyhow."

At this announcement a scream proceeded from Mrs. Latham's room, and John rushed back to her room door to reassure and comfort his mother.

"No, no, you must not go; they will kill you," moaned Mrs. Latham, clinging to her only child, and clad only in her night attire. "A fearful presentiment of evil has taken possession of me, already. Please don't leave me, my dear, darling boy."

"But, mother, they will burst down the door and take me, anyway," said John, kissing his frightened mother affectionately, "and it will be better for me to go voluntarily."

"Oh, no, my child, you must not go," sobbed the poor mother. "They will kill you, I know they will. We must barricade the door and not let them in."

"But, mother, we can't barricade the door," answered John despairingly. "Don't you hear their massive forms against the door already?"

"Yes, but I will place against it all the affections of a mother's heart for her only child," answered Mrs. Latham, still clinging to the neck of her son. "Surely, God will not let them take my only child and kill him!"

"Look here, old woman," came the gruff voice of a white man from the outside; "we've stood out here and listened to that foolishness long enough. Open this here door, or we'll bust it down, and take you along, too, and hang you with your darling boy, as a female Ku-Klux. I guess the boy inherited some of his mean-ness from you, anyway, and it would be nothin' but right to swing you up with him."

At this Mrs. Latham fainted, and after placing her gently on a sofa in the room and partially restoring her to consciousness, John opened the door to prevent the outlaws on the outside from tearing it off the hinges.

"Gentlemen, you see the condition I am in," said John, as four white men, headed by Dick Madison, came rushing into the room. "My mother has fainted, and I have not yet been able to fully restore her to conscious-ness."

"Well, what have we got to do with that matter?" asked the same grim-visaged white monster who had spoken before. "We didn't want the old woman, in particular; and, besides, we are not physicians, and if the old hag wants to faint why, let her to do it."

"Don't call my mother a hag!" said John, striking the defamer a blow between the eyes, which sent him whirling across the room.

"D—n you! I'll pay you for that," growled the shaggy-whiskered soldier, as he picked himself up and hurried back to where John was bending over his poor mother. "Bind him, boys, and let's take him to the Captain and tell him the d—d Ku-Klux struck one of his men. Old Cross-eyed Telf will fix him, I'll warrant."

"Surely, Dick," said John, appealing to the only one in the crowd whom he recognized, "you are not going to force me to leave my mother in that condition," and he pointed as he spoke to the prostrate form on the sofa.

"I'se got nothin' ter do wid it," answered Dick. "I simply obeys my orders, dat's all."

"But you can prevail on them to wait with me until mother recovers," answered John.

"No, he can't," said the shaggy-bearded rascal, whom John had just knocked down, as he proceeded to tie a rope around John's neck.

"Cross-eyed Telf told us to tie you, if you proved obstreperous, and I reckon he meant for us to prepare you for hangin', for that's what we'll do with you—at least if I have my way about it."

Just as they were leading John out of the room-door, with the rope fastened about his neck, Mrs. Latham recovered consciousness, and seeing her poor boy led

away by a rope, she uttered another wild scream and
fainted again.   This time the neighbors were aroused
by the noise, and came hurrying in, to find Mrs. Latham
lying in a swoon upon the floor, to which she had tumbled off the sofa, and no one else about the house. Restoratives were hastily sent for and applied, and she
soon regained her senses enough to moan bitterly, " Oh,
my poor boy, my poor darling boy !   They have killed
him !   They have murdered him !   They have hung
him to a tree !"

This was all the neighbors could induce her to say
during the whole of the remainder of the night, as she
lay tossing on the bed in a delirium of suffering it was
painful to see.   They could only guess from this that
something terrible had happened to John, but what it
was, or where he had gone, they tried in vain to learn.

"Aha! I see they had to tie you to induce you to
come with them," said Cross-eyed Telf, as the five soldiers appeared, leading John Latham by the rope
around his neck.

" Yes," answered Husky Diggs, " and the d—d Ku-
Klux showed fight. He actually struck *me*. See here!"
and Husky Diggs pointed his Captain to the knot between his eyes.

Husky Diggs was a short, stout, low-browed, shaggy-
whiskered scoundrel, and as he was a fair specimen of
the ragamuffin mercenaries whom the Governor hired
and placed under the command of the notorious bandit,
Cross-eyed Telf, to maltreat the good citizens of West
county and help carry the election of 1870, I will not
attempt to describe any more of them, but will let this

summary description of Husky Diggs suffice for the whole crew. He was called "Husky Diggs" because his voice was low and husky, but what his real given name was, I have never taken the trouble to inquire. He was as profane, vulgar, dirty, lousy and dishonest as the average member of the motley company commanded by Cross-eyed Telf, and that is saying a great deal to those who lived in West county and remember the stirring times of 1870.

"And the young Ku-Klux rascal resisted by force, did he ?" said Cross-eyed Telf, surveying the handsome young fellow critically, though John Latham, like Weston, thought all the time he was looking in another direction. " I guess we will be able to teach you a little better manners than that before you reach home again."

"I am ready to return at once," answered John, boldly. " I left my mother critically ill and I wish to be allowed to return to her assistance."

"Oh, don't be in too great a hurry," answered Cross-eyed Telf. "As I have just said, we wish to teach you a little good manners, and will be obliged to detain you awhile for that purpose."

"I suppose I can, at least, be informed of the cause of my arrest ?" said John, looking straight at the man, who, it seemed, never returned the look.

"Oh, certainly," answered Cross-eyed Telf. " You are arrested for the murder of Mr. Jasper Fontell !"

John's face blanched, but only for a moment.

"I know nothing about the death of Mr. Fontell," he answered, "and you have undoubtedly arrested the

10

wrong man, and with this assurance I hope you will release me, and let me return to my mother."

"Oh, just hold on a minute," answered Cross-eyed Telf. "Perhaps we can prove a little more against you than you anticipate; don't be in too great a hurry, I tell you again."

"Then, I have to say that any evidence connecting me with that unfortunate affair is false," said John, looking boldly at the awkward being before him.

"And even if we should admit that," answered Cross-eyed Telf, what can you say as to the guilt of others?"

"I have no information as to the perpetrators of that horrible crime," answered John.

"Perhaps you know, but refuse to tell," said Cross-eyed Telf.

"I tell you, positively, I know nothing in the world about the murder," answered John.

"Do you not belong to Ku-Klux-Klan No. 40?" asked Cross-eyed Telf.

For the first time John faltered and hesitated.

"Oh, we have the proof positive against you on that score," said Cross-eyed Telf, "and there is no use in trying to deny your connection with the Klan."

"Then, there can be no necessity for making me confess it," answered John.

"You might show, by answering it in the affirmative, that you were willing to confess the truth," answered Cross-eyed Telf. "I see you try to prevaricate, and I suppose we would better stop that foolishness at once. I tell you, I have sent for you for the purpose of finding out the murderers of Mr. Jasper Fontell, and you had just as well out with it at once."

"I repeat that I know nothing about the matter," said John.

"You lie about that," answered Cross-eyed Telf. "You know all about it, and I want you to understand, now, that I am going to make you disclose the facts before I turn you loose. I will try you by court-martial and hang you for the murder yourself, or make you tell."

"And if you should convict me, it would be on perjured testimony,' answered John, "for I tell you I have no idea who committed the crime, and have nothing to confess as against myself, and no testimony to give against others."

"I just now told you that was a lie!" answered Cross-eyed Telf, emphatically, "and I don't want to hear it any more."

"Husky Diggs," said Cross-eyed Telf, after a few moments' reflection, "adjust the rope a little tighter around this young man's neck, and you and the others who brought him here, follow me to the woods and we will make him disgorge or pay the penalty himself."

Then again this proud and handsome young man was led, like a dog, through the streets of his native town, and none dared to interfere and lift a hand to release him, for fear of the military mob in charge of him. It is true, at this late hour the streets were completely deserted, for a panic of fear had settled on the inhabitants, and everybody retired behind barred doors as soon as night set in. On ordinary occasions, a single cry of distress from him would have brought the whole town to his rescue; but now it was useless, and

in fact dangerous to make an alarm, for all were powerless to help.

Arrived at the woods, the rope was thrown over a
limb of a tree and John was asked if he was then
ready to tell about the murder of Fontell.

"I tell you, again, I have nothing to disclose," answered John.

"Swing him up!" ordered Cross-eyed Telf, and Huskey Diggs, assisted by the reverend Dick Madison and
the others, drew him slowly up to about three feet
above the ground.

The fearful contortions of his face and limbs, as he
struggled and strangled there in the air, as seen even
by the gentle light of the stars, were enough to have
softened the heart of a demon, but his inhuman tor-
turers looked on as complacently as if they were doing
him an act of real kindness.

Cross-eyed Telf struck a match and looked at the
young man's face carefully for a moment, and then, as
he saw his face growing purple, the order was given to
let him down. Restoratives had been prepared and
were applied freely; and, yet, it was fully five minutes
before the young man showed signs of returning life,
and fully a quarter of an hour before he attempted to
speak.

"Now tell us who killed old Fontell," demanded Cross-
eyed Telf, as soon as the young man could utter a word.

"Don't know," he gasped feebly, grabbing his lac-
erated throat as he spoke.

"You lie, you d—n Ku-Klux!" growled Cross-eyed
Telf in reply. "I tell you, I am going to have this

thing out of you or leave your body swinging to this limb to-night."

"Don't kill me," he gasped again; "I don't know."

"Swing him up again!" ordered Cross-eyed Telf, and Husky Diggs again pulled him on his feet.

"Now, are you ready to tell us?" was again demanded before suspending him from the ground.

"I have nothing to tell," answered John, and again Husky Diggs pulled the rope.

Poor John was too much exhausted to make any effort to extricate himself this time, and he hung for a few moments limp and motionless.

Cross-eyed Telf struck another match and looked at his face.

"Down, you blundering idiots!" he shouted; "I believe he is dead!"

The rope was quickly unfastened from about his neck, and he was stretched at full length upon the ground. The restoratives were again applied, and he was rubbed vigorously, but all in vain. His eyes rolled back and became set in their sockets; his lips murmured the name, that to the last moment of his life thrilled his heart, "Minnie," and then his under jaw dropped, and he was dead!

For a few minutes the murderers stood gazing at the lifeless form before them in mute astonishment. They had not intended to kill him, and were horror-struck at their blunder. At last the heartless Husky Diggs broke the silence.

"My God! it seemed that the young Ku-Klux died mighty easy."

"Yes, you d—n scoundrel," answered Cross-eyed

Telf; " you had that rope tied too tight, and I believe you did it on purpose, because he struck you when arrested."

" Oh, no, I didn't, Captain," answered Husky Diggs' beginning to quake with guilty fear; " I simply tightened it when you told me to, before leaving town."

The Captain remembered that this was so, and so said nothing in reply.

" Gentlemen," said Dick Madison, after a long pause, " it 'pears ter me we're in a fix. What er we gwine ter do wid him, now ?"

" Why, bury him, of course, you black idiot !" said Husky Diggs. " You don't suppose we are going to publish our blunder in the newspapers, do you ?"

" No, I didn't 'spose dat," answered Dick; " but I tell you it's er mighty risky bizness we're in, if his mudder ever comes to, an' 'members who it was dat took him away."

" You are right about that, Dick," said Cross-eyed Telf, " and I propose to return to town and get counsel on this matter before doing anything about it."

Accordingly they all hastened back into Westville, Husky Diggs and the others returning to their barracks as if nothing unusual had happened, while Cross-eyed Telf proceeded immediately to Weston's room at the hotel.

" Hello, this is a timely visit," said Weston, as he opened his room-door in answer to the announcement of the name of Captain Tellefson on the outside. " What in the world can be the matter ?"

" Matter enough," answered Cross-eyed Telf, as he pushed his way into the room. " We've killed the young man."

" Who ?"

"John Latham."

"And how ?"

"Why," answered Cross-eyed Telf, "we undertook to torture him, by hanging, and to make him give us the names of the murderers of Mr. Fontell, and we let him hang too long and killed him. I half believe, though, that Husky Diggs made the rope too tight on purpose."

"Any reason for believing so ?" asked Weston.

"Yes, they said Latham struck him when first arrested."

"Very likely, then," answered Weston; "but what are you going to do with the dead man ?"

"That is exactly what I have come to ask you," answered Cross-eyed Telf. "We left him lying on the ground under the tree, where we hung him, for the present,"

"Very good," answered Weston, "and is that in the woods ?"

"Yes," answered Cross-eyed Telf, "about forty yards from the road."

"And did anybody else know you had him out ?" asked Weston.

"His mother, and perhaps others, know that he was taken to my quarters at the court-house," answered Cross-eyed Telf; "but I hardly think anyone knows about our taking him to the woods or torturing him."

Weston turned the light in his lamp a little higher, as if he hoped to brighten his mental as well as physical vision and answered, after a few moments' reflection: "That is all right. Now let me tell you what to do: Go back and hide the body until to-morrow night, and then hang it to a limb near enough to the road for him to be discovered next day. In the meantime, to-morrow, tell only a few reliable men that young Latham peached on the Ku-Klux, and told you who the murderers of Old Fontell were. Next day, when his body is discovered hanging to a tree, it will be an easy matter to say that he was hanged by the Ku-Klux for disclosing their secrets and giving away the slayers of Fontell."

"That is a capital idea," answered Cross-eyed Telf, "and worthy of a lawyer. But how shall we account for his absence during the day, to-morrow?"

"Oh, that is easy enough, too," answered Weston. "Tell these same reliable persons, that certain members of Klan No. 40 secretly followed young Latham when he was first arrested, and overheard the conversation in which he gave the names of Fontell's murderers, and that, on discovering the eavesdroppers, he hid himself in the woods during the next day, fearing the violence that finally overtook him, and that the Ku-Klux found him next night (to-morrow night now) and hung him for peaching on them. Mind, you must let it be known to-morrow that he is in hiding in the woods, and you might have one of your own reliables to see him during the day and converse with him in the woods. This will help substantiate the theory that he was killed by the Ku-Klux a night later."

Crossed-eyed Telf was so delighted with Weston's shrewd solution of the difficulty that his eyes, which had never been properly set in his head, fairly danced with glee, and he left the room with many protestations of his admiration for his adviser and appreciation of his kindness. It was now much past midnight, and Crossed-eyed Telf hurriedly commissioned Husky Diggs and the others who had participated in the murder of Latham, to go back and conceal the body carefully until next night.

"Aha!" muttered Weston to himself, as he extinguished the light in his room and retired again to bed, "the caldron begins to boil more violently than I expected; but trust me to keep it stirred. I must see Tinklepaugh in the morning."

All next day Mrs. Latham lay deliriously tossing to and fro on her bed, and muttering the name of her boy. Her language was so incoherent that the neighbors and friends who had gathered in to minister to her wants were still unable to form any definite idea as to the fate of the young man; and, consequently, on the following day when his body was found suspended to a limb in the woods, and it was reported that the Ku-Klux had killed him for giving away their secrets, these same friends very rationally concluded that Mrs. Latham's unintelligible mutterings referred to the seizure of the young man by the Ku-Klux. The human mind takes great delight in solving the mysterious, and if only a slight clue is furnished as a starting point, every person you meet adds what, in his opinion, is a ray of light, if not a complete solution of the whole problem. Hence it was that Mrs. Latham's friends took great delight in confirming the report that John Latham was hanged by the Ku-Klux; and the report was soon current, and it was generally believed, that Mrs. Latham herself had said that the Ku-Klux took him off.

Such a state of excitement was never before known in the whole community, nor, indeed, in the State. The whole structure of society was heaved to its deepest depths, and fear seized the stoutest hearts. John Latham's death following so closely that of Jasper Fontell, and being, according to current rumor, so intimately connected with it, sent a thrill of terror into the heart of every man, woman and child in the community, and made them quake with fear.

This atrocious crime furnished the material out of which the two little villains spun another lengthy thread of falsehood, which was immediately sent to the aforesaid Northern looms, and by them woven into a black cloth of misrepresentation. And members of both branches of Congress, and others still higher in the councils of the nation, made themselves garments of this cloth, and wore them in the discharge of their official duties. Judges of courts made their official robes out of it, and flaunted them in the faces of litigants. Verily, truth was crushed to earth.

The following is an account of the death of John Latham, as it appeared in the *Westville Republican,* edited by the noble Peter Tinklepaugh:

"ANOTHER KU-KLUX MURDER!

" ANARCHY REIGNS SUPREME IN WEST COUNTY!

" The State Militia Powerless to Protect Citizens!

" THE AID OF FEDERAL TROOPS A NECESSITY!

"Early yesterday morning the lifeless body of Mr. John Latham was found swinging to a limb of a tree near the public road leading into the town of Westville from Kenneth Grove. The murder of Mr. Latham is evidently a sequel to the hanging of Mr. Jasper Fontell, that occurred only a few days ago, the excitement over which had not subsided when the community was again startled by the report of this last Ku-Klux outrage.

"It was generally believed, indeed, it was not doubted, that the Ku-Klux were responsible for the untimely death of Mr. Fontell, and it now appears that the murder of Mr. Latham forms another link in the chain of evidence connecting that lawless organization with the former outrage. We have it on reliable authority that Mr. Latham had become so conscience-stricken over the murder of Mr. Fontell by the Klan to which he, Latham, belonged that he turned informer, and that he was murdered by the Klan for disclosing its secrets. Mr. Latham, we are informed, was not an actual participant in the hanging of Mr. Fontell; indeed, it seems he was too upright and conscientious to be guilty of such a horrible crime, but he belonged to the Klan, and was in possession of the fatal secret, and because he was too honest to keep secret the bloody work of the lawless assassins and thereby partake of their guilt, he lost his life.

"The murder of this young man, simply because he was too good to be a murderer himself, makes the nature of the crime so shocking that we forbear to offer any comment, not being able to do the subject justice.

"Anarchy reigns supreme in this county, and the State troops are utterly powerless to deal with the situation.

"Citizens are hanged like felons for their political opinions, and those who refuse to protect the murderers share the same fate. Ku-Kluxism is the legitimate off-spring of the rebellion, and is the climax of anarchy.

"This last Ku-Klux murder, committed as it was almost in the very shadow of the court-house in which the State troops are stationed, shows that our State militia is inadequate to deal with the powerful Klan, and that nothing can stay the bloody hand of lawlessness in our midst except the interference of the general government. It seems to us that if the President longer delays sending Federal troops to this distracted county he ought to be held morally responsible for the bloody work of the Ku-Klux."

CHAPTER XII.

THE KLAN MEETS.

On the evening succeeding the funeral of John Latham, the Klan had a called meeting for the purpose of considering the charges of murder preferred against the members of the Klan by the spinners and weavers in charge of the outrage looms, and, as these charges involved the safety as well as the honor of the members, there was a full attendance. The meeting, however, was an informal one, the investigation of the charges not coming under any head of routine business, so the rigid rules of debate prescribed and adopted by the Klan were suspended, and consequently all the members participated freely in the discussion, in conversational style.

"Gentlemen," said Major Wyland, who was seated on a rude slab, "we all know that the charge that members of this Klan committed these two murders is absolutely false, but the accusation is seriously made by our enemies, and, as it has been acted upon by those high in authority, as shown by the declaration of the Governor that this county is in a state of insurrection, I think it is incumbent upon us to repel the charge, and furnish proof of our innocence."

"I thought you lawyers had a rule that no one is required to produce evidence of his innocence until he is indicted and there is some evidence of his guilt," said Sam Washburn.

"And so we have," answered Major Wyland; "but in this case we have not only been already indicted, but we have actually been convicted, and that, too, without being allowed a day in court."

"I had not thought of that," answered Sam, "and, yet, it is only too true for us to feel comfortable over the reflection."

"Yes, and if they can go that far without making any investigation as to the truth of the charges, it may be that they will actually indict us in court," said Henry Worthel.

"No, I do not apprehend any trouble of that kind," answered Major Wyland ; "and, yet, for myself, I can say that I would welcome such an indictment, because it would furnish me an opportunity to vindicate my character."

"And, yet, the murderers of Old Stingy Jap cunningly devised a scheme that furnishes some suspicious evidence against us," said Albert Seaton.

"The wretches were simply after his money," answered Sam.

"That is very evident," said Major Wyland, "and, yet, as Albert says, their scheme was deeply laid, and the circumstances and surroundings furnish to those who know nothing about the Ku-Klux some strong evidence against the Klan."

"But everybody knows Old Stingy Jap was not an offensive partisan," answered Sam, "and there could have been no object in killing him, except robbery, and the Ku-Klux is not a band of robbers."

"They have been accused of robbery quite frequently, though," said Henry Worthel.

"And every other crime in the catalogue," answered

Albert, "and, yet, it is purely a political organization, and the vast majority of the members would scorn such a thought."

"However, true that may be," answered Major Wyland, "we are accused of murder now, and it behooves us to prepare for the worst, for there is no telling what extreme measures may be resorted to by the Republicans in order to carry the next election."

"I agree with you that it is getting time for us to begin to prepare for our defence, in case of necessity," said Albert, "though it is very evident to any one acquainted with the rules of the Klan, that these murders could not have been committed by the Ku-Klux."

"Yes," answered Major Wyland, "as has already been suggested, Stingy Jap was not an active partisan, and could not have been obnoxious to the Ku-Klux on that account, and as his only besetting sin was his penuriousness, no Klan would have killed him for that. And there are many other reasons for saying that his murderers were not genuine Ku-Klux, according to the testimony before the coroner's inquest before the retirement of the jury, notwithstanding the testimony that they wore genuine Ku-Klux disguises. In the first place, the witnesses testified that the murderers were heard talking on the road to and from the home of Stingy Jap; but every Ku-Klux knows that only one person is allowed to speak while on a raid, and he must be appointed for that purpose before starting. In the second place, it is a rule of the Ku-Klux never to give any warning sign, such as hideous paintings on the door, when it is intended to inflict the death penalty;

while in this instance nearly all the representations designed as notices were used by the murderers of Fontell. Again, these admonitions are never placed on the door on the same night any punishment is inflicted, but are put there several nights, and even months, sometimes, beforehand, to warn the offender that he must desist from some objectionable practices, while in the case of Stingy Jap, we have the positive evidence of reliable persons who were at the house on the evening preceding the hanging, that no such characters were on the door then. Besides, the death penalty is not allowed to be inflicted except as a last resort, and then only after repeated warnings to the offender that he must leave the community, and in this case no previous warnings were given."

"Why not let the world know these things," asked Henry Worthel, "and so dispel the cloud of suspicion against us?"

"That is impossible," answered Major Wyland. "It would be a violation of our oath never to disclose the secrets and rules of the Klan. The general law of the Empire forbids it."

"What shall we do, then?" asked Henry.

"Well, that is for the Klan to say," answered Major Wyland. "We have met here for consultation, and to try and devise some plan by which we may establish our innocence, in case we should be arrested for murder. Perhaps our ingenious spy can suggest some line of policy to be pursued."

"No," answered Sam, "I have no plan to suggest; but we all look to you for advice in this matter. You are accustomed to giving counsel, and these matters are beyond my ken."

" Well," answered Major Wyland, " I would suggest that we all constitute ourselves detectives, and that we look out for every clue that might lead to the discovery of the real murderers of Fontell and John Latham."

" But how shall we proceed," asked Albert, " when we have no starting point? Can you not indicate some way in which we might begin our detective work?"

" Well," answered Major Wyland, " in the case of Fontell, robbery was evidently the object of his murderers, and I would suggest that we keep a sharp lookout for persons who spend money freely and who have not the means of making it rapidly. In the second place, it is said that he had a large number of State bonds on hand, and I would recommend that some member of our Klan be sent to the office of the Secretary of State, with instructions to examine the records there and take the number and date of the bonds issued to Jasper Fontell. The law requires the State Treasurer to keep, in a book prepared for that purpose, a memorandum of every bond of the State issued by the State, together with the numbers, date of issue, when and where payable, at what premium, and to whom the same may have been sold or issued. The Treasurer can then be instructed to note the person who presents the bonds for payment, or for the payment of interest, and in this way we may be able to discover the possessor of the bonds."

" But perhaps the State Treasurer would not be willing to assist in detecting the murderers," suggested

11

Henry; "especially if they proved to be party favorites."

"Oh, I hardly think our Treasurer would refuse a request of that kind," answered Major Wyland, "and if he should, we could make his refusal defeat him in the next election, and we would then get a man who would assist us."

"But suppose the bonds are transferred to another person?" said Sam.

"Then the law requires the surrender and cancellation of the bonds," answered Major Wyland, "and new bonds for the same amount to be issued to the transferee."

"And in the case of the murder of John Latham, what do you suggest?" asked Sam, pleased with the ingenuity displayed by the old lawyer.

"In that case," answered Major Wyland, "I recommend that some member of the Klan, or what would perhaps be better, that some female friend be permitted to remain in the room with Mrs. Latham until she recovers, and it may be that even in her delirious ravings she may let fall some word that would furnish a clue as to the identity of his murderers."

Mrs. Latham had remained completely demented ever since the night John was torn from her side, and as no one else had seen the military ruffians in charge of him, or knew anything about their taking him off, the report circulated by Cross-eyed Telf, to the effect that the Ku-Klux had killed him for betraying the murderers of old Jasper Fontell, had been generally accepted as true. Indeed, some of the strongest Democrats in the community were beginning to condemn the existence of the Klan as a band of murderous assassins. They had hitherto winked at the little misdeeds of the Klan—such as whipping a negro, a carpet-bagger, or a scalawag for being too active in political matters; but that they should commit murder in carrying out the designs of the Ku-Klux, and then kill one of their own number for exposing their hellish deeds, was just a little more than the public conscience could stand, and so the righteous indignation of the whole country was aroused against the Klan. And the members of the Klan felt very keenly the sting of the stigma thus cast upon them. The Klan was composed of some of the best men in the whole country, who had joined it simply for the purpose of destroying the Union Leagues and overthrowing the reign of the carpet-baggers by gentler means than the taking of life, and they shuddered at the thought of being charged with murder.

Having mutually agreed to assist and defend each other in case of necessity, and to act as detectives in trying to discover the perpetrators of the crimes with which the members were charged, the Klan dispersed and the members returned to their homes, feeling very much mortified at the turn affairs had taken and their inability to ferret out the true facts.

CHAPTER XIII.

A CONFLICT OF AUTHORITY.

On the morning of the 20th of July, 1870, Major
Wyland was sitting in his elegantly furnished office
on Main street in the town of Westville, when a boy
rapped at the door, and, being admitted, handed him
a large sealed envelope. Judging hastily by the bulk
and weight of the package that it contained only some
legal documents, which he had sent for the evening
before to be brought from the office of the Superior
Court Clerk, he was about to lay it unopened on the
table before him, to be opened and examined at his
leisure, when the messenger accosted him with the
remark :

"He said to let him know at once whether you could
come, and if you couldn't come right now, to come as
soon as possible."

Hastily tearing open the envelope, he was startled at
finding that it contained in fact a legal document, though
not the one he had sent for, but one which emanated
from a court he thought and hoped had vanished with
the last roar of belligerent cannons. A short note
enclosed first attracted his attention, the contents of
which were as follows :

"*My Dear Major Wyland:* I have been arrested by
the military authorities, and am now imprisoned in one
of the rooms of the court-house. I send you the copy
of the papers served on me, which contains all the
information I have received as to the cause of my
arrest.

" Please come to me at once, and let me know if any legal process can be sued out to secure my liberation.

    "Yours very truly,   Albert Seaton.

" July 20, 1870."

"Did you wish to take an answer back ?" asked Major Wyland, as he laid the note on the table before proceeding to the examination of the more lengthy document.

" He said to bring a reply, unless you could answer at once in person," answered the intelligent looking boy who had brought the message.

" I will answer, in person, immediately after examining the papers," said Major Wyland ; " so you need not wait for a reply."

Left alone again, Major Wyland read carefully and critically the following interesting document, which is given as a specimen exhibition of the grinding military despotism practiced upon the people of West county during the summer of 1870 :

" Headquarters Department of ....,

    "*Division Embracing West County,*

        "July 20th, 1870.

" General Court Martial, Orders No. 1.

"Before a Military Commission convened at Westville, July 20th, 1870, under authority received from Headquarters Department ...., there was arraigned and tried : Albert Seaton, citizen.

"charge :

"For publishing and circulating disloyal and seditious writings within a district under martial law.

"*Specification.*—In this, that the said Albert Seaton, citizen, of West county, State of ...., and editor of a newspaper named and known as the *Westville Conservative*, published at Westville, in said county and State, did publish in said newspaper, and circulate an article in words as follows:

"'As a public journalist we feel constrained to enter our protest against the action of our Governor in declaring West county to be in a state of insurrection. His establishment of martial law for this county was an unwarranted exercise of the dangerous power vested in him by that unconstitutional and slanderous statute known as the Ku-Klux Act. It is true there have been several trivial outrages committed in the county, and lately we have had perpetrated in our midst two most atrocious murders; but we assert positively, and we are willing to stake our reputation for veracity on the assertion, that these murders were not committed by the Ku-Klux, as alleged, but were committed by private persons for the purpose of robbery, in the one case, and possibly for revenge in the other; and we confidently believe, and so declare, that time and a thorough investigation of these crimes will prove the truth of our prediction. To have a military despot sitting as the sole arbiter of the rights of our citizens is a humiliation that is hard to bear, and our Governor is inexcusable for thrusting such a state of serfdom upon us.'

"The charge is, that said article was calculated and intended to produce hostility to the government, and cause resistance to the constituted authorities.

"To which charge and specification the accused, Albert Seaton, pleaded as follows:

" To the specification of the charge, '*guilty*', except so much as alleges that the said article was calculated and intended to produce hostility to the government and cause resistance to the constituted authorities.

" To the charge, '*not guilty.*'

" The court having maturely considered the evidence adduced finds the accused, Albert Seaton, citizen, as follows :

" Of the specification to the charge, *guilty.*

" Of the charge, *guilty.*

" SENTENCE :

" The said Albert Seaton is, therefore, sentenced to imprisonment in the jail of West county for thirty days.

" By command of Crawford Tellefson, Captain."

Major Wyland finished reading this remarkable document, and then sat for a few moments almost stupefied with astonishment. That a military subordinate, only a Captain, should issue an order for the arrest of a citizen and actually try and convict him by a court martial, of which he was the self-constituted head, and sentence him to imprisonment, was an act of despotism that stood without a parallel in the history of any enlightened nation of people. Verily, the last vestige of freedom had vanished from Southern soil, and the people were reduced to the condition of serfs. He had thought that he had foreseen the evils of the military usurpation, but he was not prepared to hear of such an unauthorized assumption of power as this.

Recovering after a few minutes from the effects of the startling news, he left his office and proceeded to

the court-house, where he was met at the door by
Husky Diggs, orderly sergeant for the day, who demanded to know his business.

"I wish to be allowed to see a client who, I understand, has been imprisoned in the court-house," he answered, casting an indignant look upon the ill-natured
visage of the man who confronted him.

"Oh, he has no use for a lawyer now," answered
Husky Diggs, "he's already convicted and in prison,
and all hell can't git him away from Cross-eyed Telf
now."

"At any rate I wish to be allowed to see him," answered Major Wyland.

"Well, I'll go and ask the Captain about it," said
Husky Diggs, and he left Major Wyland standing in
the door surrounded by a motley crowd of the band of
hoodlumns while he went in search of the Captain.
Cross-eyed Telf was never hard to find by those who
knew his habits, so Husky Diggs proceeded at once to
the "wine-room," where he found the Captain enjoying a glass of "moonshine." He had been drunk all
day; was drunk, in fact, when he issued the order for
the arrest of Albert Seaton, and there was no hope of
improving his condition much as long as the pop-skull
lasted.

"Captain," said Husky Diggs, as he poked his head
in the door, "there is an old sheep-skin thumber out
here, who wants to see the young Ku-Klux bird you
caged to-day."

"Tell him to come in and have a drink with me,"
answered Cross-eyed Telf, who by this time was unable
to rise from the keg on which he was seated.

"No," answered Husky Diggs, "he insists that he only wants to see the goslin' Ku-Klux, so I'll just swaller his share myself," and the low-browed villain drained a full glass.

"Then bring 'em both in here," said Cross-eyed Telf. "They will not be allowed to see each other except in my presence, and my presence is *here* just now." This last observation was true, as has already been explained.

Husky Diggs returned and informed Major Wyland of the orders of the Captain, and then unlocked the door of the room in which Albert was incarcerated.

"Come out, you Ku-Klux quill driver," said Husky Diggs to Albert; "there's an old jawy cross-questioner out here who wants to filch a few dollars out of you, and the Captain wishes to drink your health in the wine-room while he does it. I tell you, young man, there ain't no use in sendin' for a lawyer after old Cross-eyed Telf gits his claws on you."

Albert feared the truth of this last remark, and the thought of having to remain in that dusty room surrounded by the noise of the tramping, the vulgarity, and the swearing indulged in by the boorish military hirelings about him, made him faint at heart; but, still, at the announcement of Major Wyland's appearance, he arose with alacrity from the rough bench on which he had been reclining, and followed his swarthy conductor to the presence of his counsel. The sight of no person on earth is ever more welcome than the appearance of a lawyer, who comes as the legal adviser to a condemned prisoner. The invalid, racked with pain and scorched with fever, as he rolls restlessly from one side of his bed to the other, listens eagerly for the sound of his physician's footsteps, and swallows submissively the bitter potion he administers. But in the case of the sick man it is only his own physical infirmity that confines him, and he feels so long as any hope of recovery survives that the pain will ere long exhaust itself, and the burning fever subside, even without the assistance of the doctor's medicines; while on the other hand, the imprisoned captive realizes that his environments are all external and beyond his control; he feels, too, especially an innocent prisoner, that all that is necessary to secure his release is to convince the minds of his persecutors of his innocence by satisfactory argument, or to reach their hearts by persuasive entreaty; but he knows that his own efforts have already proved unavailing, and his heart yearns for the aid of an advocate more eloquent and powerful than himself. The fact is that we are all dependent children, and remain so as long as we live, and our hearts are ever yearning for the counsel of a wiser voice and the guidance of a stronger hand than our own. Then the sight of prison walls, viewed from the inside, brings with it a pang of humilitation more intolerable than any fever or pain.

Husky Diggs conducted Major Wyland and Albert to the wine-room, where they found Cross-eyed Telf still sitting on the keg of blockade, for this military satrap respected not even the revenue laws, but purchased his liquor from the blockade-runners because it was cheaper. By this time he was cleverly drunk.

"Have a sheat shennlemens," said the thick-tongued scoundrel, looking, as Major Wyland thought, directly at a barrel of brandy on the opposite side of the room.

"No," answered Major Wyland, looking around and seeing nothing on which he could sit, except a few kegs and barrels of "mountain dew," and not caring to imitate the drunken beast before him in any particular; "I have simply called to inquire into the cause of the arrest and detention of this young man."

"Court's over," answered Cross-eyed Telf. "Have a drink, shennlemens, Husky Diggs, (hic) pour the shennlemens out a drink."

"No, I thank you," answered Major Wyland, as Husky Diggs began to fill the room with the offensive odor of the distilled moonshine; "I do not care for a drink just now; but I would like to inquire if this case has been finally disposed of."

"Yes," answered the drunken sot on the keg.

"Then I would like to inquire further, if you are sober enough to tell me," said Major Wyland, "by what authority you have arrested and imprisoned him."

"By my own (hic) s'preme power," answered Cross-eyed Telf indignantly, and he attempted to rise as he spoke in order to emphasize the declaration of his authority, but "the ardent" proved stronger than his muscles, and he tumbled over between two kegs and lay there prostrate upon his face, unable to extricate himself.

"I see there is no use in spending our time with this maudlin wretch," said Major Wyland, turning and speaking to Albert; "so I will return to my office and prepare a writ of *habeas corpus* to test the validity of your imprisonment."

"And what's a writ of *habis corpis?*" asked Husky Diggs.

"It is a writ by which we hope to take the body of your prisoner from you," answered Major Wyland contemptuously.

"Oh, his corpse," answered the low-browed ruffian. "Why, you can have his carcass any time you'll send a cart around for it. We have plenty of men here who will dress it up for you in regular Ku-Klux style."

"Never mind the threats of the base-born varlet," said Major Wyland to Albert, seeing the blanched countenance of the young man. "I will prepare an application for a writ of *habeas corpus* immediately, and I think I can secure your release."

"But suppose Judge Farwell should refuse to grant the writ," said Albert despairingly.

"He dare not refuse it," answered Major Wyland. "The law imposes a heavy penalty on a judge for such refusal."

"But he has already decided against me in one case," said Albert, remembering with a shudder the decision of Judge Farwell in the famous salt case; "and by that judgment he reduced me to extreme poverty."

"That was in a civil case," answered Major Wyland, trying to console the disconsolate youth, "and the law guards the liberties of citizens more sacredly that the rights of property, though I must confess that the argus-eyed Goddess of Liberty appears to be very remiss in her duty at present."

"Time's up," said Husky Diggs, who understood just enough of this conversation to surmise that the old lawyer was going to make some effort to liberate his prisoner; so he took Albert by the arm and conducted him back to his cell, while Major Wyland returned to his office. After locking Albert in, Husky Diggs returned to his drunken master, and lifting him up and finding him unable to either stand or sit, he laid him prostrate on the floor, and then proceeded to fill himself up with liquor.

"I wish to present an application for a writ of *habeas corpus*," said Major Wyland, as he entered Judge Farwell's office an hour later.

"Pray, be seated Major," answered Judge Farwell, as he rose politely and accepted the document.

Resuming his seat, the Judge hastily glanced over the application, which contained a verified copy of all the papers relating to the case by virtue of which Albert Seaton had been arrested and imprisoned.

"My God!" exclaimed Judge Farwell, when he had finished reading the remarkable document; "has it come to this, that a citizen can be arrested and sentenced to prison by a contemptible drumhead court martial, the head of which is only a Captain of militia?"

"It seems that such a thing has actually happened," answered Major Wyland complacently.

"Well, this is the most revolutionary usurpation of unauthorized power that has ever come under my observation," answered the Judge as he took his pen and signed the writ prayed for. "I will readily grant the writ, and I doubt if that ancient and stable bulwark of our liberties has ever been more providently issued since the memorable scene at Runny-Mede."

"It is, indeed, loudly called for in this instance," answered Major Wyland, pleased at the view taken of the matter by Judge Farwell.

"And how does Albert bear up under the sentence?" asked the Judge.

"He seems very much humiliated and depressed," answered Major Wyland.

"I do not wonder at it," said the Judge. "The indignity thus heaped upon him is none the less hard to bear because it is unlawful. I am very much surprised that such a ruffian as Cross-eyed Telf should be placed in charge of a company of troops; but I think, after this exhibition of his ignorance and cruelty, I will not manifest any astonishment at anything further he may do."

"I am very much surprised myself that the troops should have been ordered here at all," answered Major Wyland. "There was no necessity for declaring this county in a state of insurrection.

"I agree with you in that opinion," answered Judge Farwell, "and I say to you seriously, though I have no doubt you will be greatly astonished to learn it, that the illegal means resorted to by the Republican party, in order to secure a victory at the coming election, has caused me to resolve to sever my connection with that party forever."

"Why, I am astonished to hear such a declaration," answered Major Wyland. "To be candid with you, though, since your avowal of a change of heart, you may not think me very complimentary, I thought you were in full sympathy with the party, even in its wildest excesses."

"Your opinion does me great injustice, as applied to my present state of feeling," answered Judge Farwell, "though I must confess that I have been in the past in full accord with that party in most of its measures. I had been raised a Republican, and had been taught from a child that Democracy meant hostility to the government; in fact, the word in my infantile vocabulary was synonymous with rebellion and treason. But I have discovered at last, to my sorrow, that the Republican party in the South is not composed of the same material as at the North. Up North that party embraces the best classes of society, while down here it is composed of the lowest elements. I cannot longer remain in a party that I see is every day plunging the State into bankruptcy, and that seeks to sustain its waning power by the use of the bayonet, and I have determined to announce publicly my withdrawal from such a party."

"Judge Farwell," said Major Wyland, his heart swelling with genuine emotion, "I see you have been sadly deceived, and I am glad to know that you repudiate a party that seeks to reduce our people to a state of serfdom more galling than that of the Russian slave. Now let us attend to this *habeas corpus* case, and we will discuss this matter more fully at some other time."

"I will call my office boy," said Judge Farwell, "and have him to deliver the papers to the Sheriff. I have made them returnable at noon to-day."

In answer to Judge Farwell's call, an intelligent looking negro lad came into the room and took the papers and set out at once to find the Sheriff of West county. Major Wyland also left at this time, promising to return to the Judge's office promptly at twelve o'clock. It was then eleven, and Judge Farwell spent the next hour pacing his office floor in a deep reverie.

He had felt for some time that he could not longer affiliate with a party that was evidently destroying the Commonwealth by pledging its faith to so many questionable schemes of plunder, and yet he was not insensible to the serious importance of the step he proposed to take. To turn his back on the party now, after having enjoyed its favors so long, would look like ingratitude, and yet he could not approve the action of the authorities in seeking to perpetuate their power by placing military despots in charge of the ballot-boxes. He had a sincere reverence for all lawfully constituted authority, but a supreme contempt for all illegal usurpation, and he felt that the action of Cross-eyed Telf in arresting Albert Seaton was an outrage in itself enough to cause any lover of liberty to leave a party responsible for his action.

He was aroused from his reverie by the appearance of the Sheriff at the door.

"Cross-eyed Telf is drunk, Judge," said the Sheriff, "and Husky Diggs refuses to deliver up his prisoner."

"Is Captain Tellefson too drunk to make any return to the writ," asked the Judge.

"I presume he is," answered the Sheriff; "at any rate he has directed Husky Diggs not to respect the writ, and to refuse to let Albert go."

"Then it is your duty to take him by force," answered Judge Farwell, "and you may call in the whole power of the county to assist you. How many men has 'Cross-eyed Telf,' as you call him?"

"About one hundred," answered the Sheriff.

"Then go back and have your deputies to assist you in summoning two hundred men, and direct them all to appear, armed with whatever instruments of war they may possess, at the court-house within an hour. Then take Albert and bring him before me if, in order to do so, you have to fill the court-house with dead troops."

Sheriff Albertson was a brave man, who only wanted to know his duty, and he would discharge it with fidelity and courage. Consequently in less time than that specified by Judge Farwell, he had a force of two hundred young men drawn up in battle array in front of the court-house. By this time Cross-eyed Telf, who had just taken a long nap, had sobered considerably, and seeing the strong opposing force under the command of the Sheriff, he began to realize to some extent the gravity of the situation, and to consider what had best be done. Husky Diggs advised that he send for counsel, and the Captain, remembering how admirably Donald Weston had extricated him from a former dilemma, immediately despatched a messenger for that sage counsellor, while he counted, as accurately as his befuddled mind would permit, the forces in front.

Weston soon appeared, and demanded to know the cause of so much disturbance and the reason for the display of so great a force.

"I have come to take a prisoner now in charge of Captain Tellefson, who refuses to deliver him up," said the Sheriff.

"And by what authority do you seek to take him out of the custody of Captain Tellefson?" demanded the little attorney.

"By virtue of a writ of *habeas corpus* issued by Judge Farwell," answered the Sheriff.

12

"But the civil authorities have no right to grant that writ—to take a person imprisoned under the final judgment of a court martial," answered Weston.

"You can make your points of law before Judge Farwell," answered the Sheriff; "but, as for my part, I intend to take the prisoner, or die in the attempt."

Weston looked at the men before him, and saw that they were well armed; in fact all the munitions of war to be found in the hardware stores of the town had been freely tendered the Sheriff and his *posse*, and most of the men were not only well equipped, but were eager for the fray, and this desire for battle was plainly visible in their stern countenances. The doughty little attorney hesitated. If he should precipitate a fight by counselling resistance to the Sheriff's *posse*, the responsibility for the result, which it was impossible to forsee, would fall principally upon him; while, on the other hand, if Tellefson should yield the custody of the prisoner, the strength and influence of the military authority would be broken, and the power upon which he relied for the promotion of his wicked schemes would vanish. If a few shots could be fired and a little blood flow in the streets, the Northern outrage looms might weave out of it a bloody shirt that could be flaunted in the faces of Southern statesmen for all time to come. Again self-interest predominated, as it always does in the breast of a really wicked man, and again the voice of Sempronius was heard declaring for war, but this time not in the Roman Senate, trying to incite resistance to the subjugator of the people; but it was the voice of a little unscrupulous demagogue, trying to stir up insurrection in order that he might feast and fatten on carnage like a vulture.

"I do not think you can afford to surrender the custody of the prisoner," said Weston, turning to Cross-eyed Telf. "The publication of that article was evidently intended to provoke opposition to your authority, and the appearance of this unusual array of force to resist your power is but the legitimate fruit of such seditious writing. You cannot surrender him without giving up your commission as Captain at the same time."

This last thrust hit the mark intended, the vanity of the Captain.

Excitement sobers a drunken man even quicker than sleep, and by this time Cross-eyed Telf had almost entirely recovered his equilibruim. He estimated that the excess in numbers of the sheriff's *posse* was more than counterbalanced by his advantageous position, so he decided to fight, and quickly gave orders that his men should station themselves in the windows and doors of the court-house, seeking the protection of the walls as much as possible, and that they should open fire on the first man who placed his feet on the door-steps.

Husky Diggs was placed at the door of the room in which Albert was imprisoned, with instructions to guard the door even at the sacrifice of his life. Having hurriedly completed his preparations for the expected battle, Cross-eyed Telf announced to the sheriff his determination to fight from a window in the second story of the building.

The sheriff's *posse* was composed mainly of hot-blooded youths from the town, who were eagerly waiting for permission from the sheriff to fire, and this

being now given, Cross-eyed Telf was immediately answered by a shot that took off his ear. A volley
quickly followed, and this was answered by a heavy
discharge from the windows and doors.

Sheriff Albertson still possessed that intrepid courage and calm judgment that so distinguished him in a
graver war than that now on hand, and he soon discovered that it was foolish to fight in that exposed
place while his enemy had the advantage of the walls
of the court-house for a protection. His quick percep-
tion took in the situation at a glance. Projecting from
the second story in front was a long piazza, or balcony,
supported by huge round pillars reaching to the ground,
and his men were immediately ordered to take shelter
under the piazza. Once under this security there were
only two windows facing them, and as these had been
imprudently left raised, the sheriff's men poured
through them so rapidly that those within were routed
and fled through the doors in confusion, without offer-
ing any further resistance. Cross-eyed Telf and the
men up stairs were now utterly powerless to do any
further fighting, and as Albert had been allowed to remain in the room below, Husky Diggs was easily over-
powered, the door torn off its hinges, and the prisoner
rescued.

Cross-eyed Telf, seeing the ridiculous mistake he had
made, and realizing the ignominious defeat he had sustained, now sent a man down to say to the sheriff that
he only yielded to superior forces, and that he still
protested against this interference with his authority.

Albert was immediately taken before Judge Farwell,
and on motion of Major Wyland, who appeared as his

counsel, was released from custody. After the order for his discharge had been properly signed and attested, Judge Farwell handed Albert a paper and remarked:

"I want you to publish this in the next issue of the *Westville Conservative.* It is a card to the public announcing my repudiation of the Republican party."

"I am very much surprised, Judge, but I assure you it does my heart good to hear it," answered Albert.

"Yes," answered Judge Farwell, "I have had this departure under advisement for some time, and after mature delibration, I have decided that I cannot afford to affiliate longer with a party that permits such outrages as your imprisonment to be carried on with impunity. I have, indeed, been thinking very seriously to day about resigning my office as Judge."

"That will not do now," answered Albert. "We may need you again soon, if the tyrannical military company remains here."

"I had thought of that," answered the Judge. "If that inhuman wretch called Cross-eyed Telf, continues in command here, there is no telling to what extremity he may go. He seems to be utterly destitute of sympathy."

"I can testify as to the truth of that, myself," answered Albert. "And, yet, I do not think he is alone responsible for all the devilment indulged in around here of late."

"You think he has an accomplice?" asked the Judge.

"Only in the capacity of an adviser and counsellor," answered Albert.

"I am really afraid your surmise is correct," said Judge Farwell reflectively. "I have noticed that Wes-

ton has shunned me for the last few days, and I am
very much afraid that he has joined Tellefson and his
coadjutors in trying to carry the approaching election
by force."

This conversation was cut short by the appearance
of a crowd of men walking past the office, carrying a
man on a litter. Albert looked out the open door, and
recognized the bloody form of Sam Washburn. Turning away with a shudder, he grasped the hand of Judge
Farwell cordially, as an eloquent expression of his appreciation of the favor shown him that day, and then
left the office without speaking a word and followed
the track of blood. The ball, they said, had perforated
one lung, but the physician entertained hopes of his
recovery. It was the most serious injury sustained by
any one in the battle at the court-house. Albert followed for some distance, but began to grow faint at the
sight, and turned back and went home to his invalid
mother.

The following was the story of the engagement at
the court-house, as woven by the outrage looms:

"WAR! WAR!! WAR!!!

"*The Ku-Klux Fire on State Troops!*

"On the 20th instant, at Westville, the Ku-Klux with
a force one thousand strong appeared in front of the
court-house, in which the State troops had been stationed by order of the Governor of that State, who
had declared West county to be in a state of insurrection, and fired upon the troops, wounding Captain
Tellefson and killing several of his men. Captain
Tellefson had a force only one hundred strong, and

the Ku-Klux, it seems, have determined to drive the troops out of the county in order that they may carry on their diabolical work of whipping negroes and murdering and robbing the wealthy and influential. No other cause is assigned for the hellish deed, even by the Ku-Klux themselves, and they openly boast that they will kill every man in the county who refuses to pledge himself to vote the Democratic ticket in the coming election. The Great Rebellion, with all its carnage, was a mercy to what the good people of West county are forced to endure at the hands of the law-defying and bloody-handed Ku-Klux. No person's life is safe, and many good people have abandoned home and everything, and are flying in terror for their lives. It is understood that the Governor will demand that a company of Federal troops be sent to the assis-ance of the State militia."

CHAPTER XIV.

THE DEATH CHAMBER.

Albert Seaton went home from his prison cell to his mother's death chamber. She had remained in a very critical condition ever since the day the sad funeral obsequies were held over the skeleton corpse of her late husband, and the fresh shock occasioned by the outrageous imprisonment of her son, and the news of the battle to secure his liberation, was more than her nervous system could bear. She had not learned the termination of the combat before Albert's arrival, and was still laboring under the impression that he would be killed by the ruffian usurpers rather than surrende him, when he approached her bedside and gently kissed her hand.

"Oh, my dear son," feebly gasped the dying woman, "I am so glad you have come. I feared I would hav to die without ever seeing you again."

"Do not talk of dying, mother," said Albert, tembling with fear as he gazed upon the feeble fame before him. "They have not hurt me, and I am orry to see you so frightened."

"It is more than fright this time," answere Mrs. Seaton. "It is the hand of death upon me, and have so much to tell you before I die."

The dying woman put both hands to her orehead and pressed her temples with all the strengt her feeble arms possessed. She seemed to be stragely agitated, and her excitement, instead of abang since

Albert's arrival, appeared to become every moment more intensified.

"I want all to leave the room," she said at last, "except Albert and Bessie, and Dr. Wyland."

This request having been complied with, she asked to be supported in a sitting posture by pillows, and this being done by the kind-hearted physician, brother of the distinguished lawyer, she took Albert and Bessie each by the hand, and, summoning all her strength for the last act in the drama of her life, thus addressed them, speaking to Bessie first:

"Bessie, my dear, sweet child, I am going to die and leave you forever, and I want to hear you call me mother once more before I go. You are my child, are you not, Bessie?"

"Yes, mother; you know I am," answered the weeping girl.

"And have I always been a good mother to you, Bessie?"

"Yes, my dear mother, you have always been extremely good and kind to me."

"And do you love me as your mother?"

"Yes, mother," answered Bessie, choking with emotion so that she could only answer the questions of the dying mother.

"And has Albert always been a good brother to you?" still querried the dying woman.

"Yes, mother."

"And do you love him?"

"Yes, mother, I love him."

"And you, Albert, do you love Bessie?"

"Yes, mother, I love her," answered Albert.

"Then listen to me, my children," and the expiring woman cast her glazy eyes first upon one and then the other as she spoke. "I have a strange and startling story to relate to you. You are not my daughter, Bessie, and Albert is not your brother. Albert is my only child. But to tell you the whole story I must begin with my own infancy. My father and mother both died when I was quite an infant, leaving me a valuable estate. My father left a will in which he appointed Mr. Arthur DeVoy executor and guardian for me, giving him the option of investing my money and of appropriating to his own use all the proceeds of such investments above legal interest, or of simply preserving the property until I became of age without having to account for interest. If he should choose the former mode, he was required to give bond for the forthcoming of my money, and interest, when I should reach my twenty-first birthday; if he should choose the latter method, no bond was required. Mr. DeVoy adopted the former method and wisely invested my money in such a way that when I attained legal age and married Mr. Seaton he was enabled to turn over to me everything that was demanded of him under the will, and to reserve for himself quite a fortune thus accumulated. Mr. DeVoy, at the time of my marriage to Mr. Seaton, was a bachelor, and when Albert was born a year afterwards, he came over to see him, and, because he was the son of his ward, he called Albert his grandson, and soon grew very fond of him, spending most of his time fondling him and buying him presents. Four years later, Mr. DeVoy married Ellen Crawford. They were our nearest neighbors, and Mr. DeVoy continued to fondle and caress my little boy, until about a year after his marriage, when his wife presented him with a daughter. Contrary to the usual custom of husbands, he manifested great joy on discovering that his offspring was a girl, and came over immediately after Albert, who was then five years old, and took him over, as he said, to see his little sweetheart. Afterwards Albert visited the house every day, and called the little girl his little sweetheart, much to the delight of her parents. Eight months later Mrs. DeVoy sickened and died, but on her death bed she made Albert promise to marry his little sweetheart when she became of age. Mr. DeVoy was overwhelmed with grief at his wife's death, but soon ended his sorrow by following her to the grave. He was a good man, but very eccentric, as all men are who live a life of celibacy up to the age of fifty, and he also made a will in which he appointed Dr. Wyland, here, his executor and guardian for his little girl. In his will, after reciting the fact that all his fortune had been acquired by investments of my money, and expressing his gratitude, he directed that his little daughter should be placed under my care and reared by me as my own daughter; that I should call her my daughter and teach her to call me mother and Albert her brother, and that she and Albert should never know but that they were brother and sister until the little girl should reach the age of twenty-one. The will further provided that in case Albert and the little girl should marry when they became grown, then all the testator's property was to go to both of them equally, but if either should wilfully refuse to marry the other, then all the property was to go to the one refused. Albert was soon taught to cease calling the little girl sweetheart, and to call her sister.

That little girl, Bessie, is yourself, and your true name is Bessie DeVoy. If you should change it to Bessie Seaton in fact, you would be carrying out the will of your deceased parents as well as the wishes of ——.''

But the effort had been too great for the dying woman, and she expired without finishing the sentence, still holding the hands of Albert and Bessie. The final esparation of soul and body appeared to take place without agony. Her tongue simply lay still in her, mouth, because there was no more breath to vibrate it. The soul simply bade adieu to the cold tenement of clay, and took its flight to the realm beyond the chilly waters of the river of death, there to rejoin the spirit of the murdered husband, and to go forth, wing bound to wing, new-born, and explore the great Unknown.

Bessie relinquished herself from the grasp of the cold, clammy hand of the dead, and retired to her room, where her grief-rent heart poured itself out in bitter tears. Death, the relentless destroyer of all human happiness, had twice made her an orphan, and the knowledge of her bereavements had come to her all at once. Fatherless, motherless, brotherless, sisterless, homeless, comfortless! She was, indeed, desolate. Imagination even refused to penetrate the dark future; her mind was benumbed with sorrow, her tongue paralizea with woe, her heart ached and throbbed with inconceivable anguish, and her soul cried: God! God! Hush! O, busy world, and listen for a moment to the moan that comes from the breast of the poor inconsolable girl!

The lamentation of the orphan girl, though unheard save by the ear of Him who ever listen to the wail of the distressed and takes care of the bereaved, was silently re-echoed in the heart of the other newly-made orphan, as he walked to and fro in the garden. It was now night, and the gentle moon looked down benignantly and compassionately into the swollen eyes of the grief-stricken young man, as he walked alone in the mellow moonlight, nursing a burning grief that could not vent itself in tears. Finding no comfort in the garden, Albert was about to return to the house when Dr. Wyland approached and took him by the arm. The good physician was like his brother only in personal appearance. Both were naturally kind-hearted, but Major Wyland had trained his mind and heart for heated controversy, and had neglected to cultivate the finer and more benignant qualities, while Dr. Wyland's whole life had been spent in trying to alleviate pain and minister to the wants of the suffering, and his voice was accustomed to uttering words of comfort to the distressed.

"This is a sad bereavement, Albert," said Dr. Wyland, as they walked the flower-lined path through the garden; "but it is one that must come sooner or later to all the living. Our parents must leave us orphans at some stage of our lives if we are permitted to live out our own allotted time."

"I know it," answered Albert, brushing away the first scalding tear that had escaped his feverish, swollen eyes; "but this is a double loss to me."

"Yes, your grief is hard to bear, I know," answered the good doctor, "but it is not greater than that of others, and you should endeavor to endure it without murmuring in order to encourage her who is equally bereft."

"Oh, please don't speak to me of my poor s—", but

the last word died unuttered on his tongue, and his sorrow now found a vent in tears.

It is well to weep under such circumstances. It is
not a hopeful symptom of improvement to see the
heart so benumbed with grief that the very fountain
of feeling becomes obstructed and stagnant. It is good
for the heart that has been wrenched violently asunder
to bleed; but at such a time the sufferer desires nothing more than solitude, and the voice of sympathy and
compassion brings but little consolation. Great griefs
must have time to flow out in tears before the heart can
be healed. Dr. Wyland recognized this truth, as he
felt the whole frame of the strong young man tremble
against his arm, so he turned to leave him alone in his
sorrow saying:

"Your affliction is great, my young friend; but God,
if you will only ask Him, will enable you to look through
this dark veil of death to a brighter and a living vision
beyond. Affliction is God's school in which he teaches
us the frailty of human things, and those only are impaired by sorrow who fail to catch the true meaning of
the lesson. Destiny, in mixing the cup of life, has stirred in it many bitter sorrows, which we must all drink
if we would taste the sweet also. These tonics are always bitter, but they are not intended to be palatable,
but healing. Only try to recognize God's hand in your
affliction, and you will find that His arm is strong and
ready to sustain."

After this the aged physician returned to the house,
and gave directions for the preparation of the funeral.

Next day they buried Mrs. Seaton, beside the grave
in which, only a few weeks before, had been interred
the bones of her murdered husband.

CHAPTER XV.

STILL WEAVING BLOODY WOOF.

" Have you seen it ?"

" Seen what ?"

" The card."

. " What card ?"

" Why, Judge Farwell's card, in which he withdraws from the Republican party and declines a re-election." And Tinklepaugh handed Weston a copy of the *Westville Conservative* and pointed to the following :

"A CARD TO THE PUBLIC.

" Recent political events which have transpired in this State, and which seem to have the approval of the leaders of the Republican party, have convinced me that it is the duty of all persons who love peace and harmony, and who desire to see the autonomy of our State preserved from the destructive rapacity of the greedy political cormorants who now have charge of the State government, to vote for the overthrow of that party in the coming election, and believing this, I have resolved to vote the Democratic ticket at the next election, and to affiliate with that party in the future.

" The policy of the Republican party in this State for the last few years has been to use the government as an instrument of plunder, and in pursuance of this policy they have levied taxes that amount practically to confiscation of private property, and that made the

tax-gatherer a highway robber. Some of the money
thus raised by exorbitant taxation, has been squandered
in unwise speculation to which the State has been made
a party, and vast sums have been used to pay special
officers for very questionable services; for instance, the
hiring of unprincipled military despots to imprison and
shoot down citizens of the State without authority of
law or shadow of right. Millions of State bonds have
been issued to build railroads that will never have any
existence, except on paper, and recently one of the presi-
dents of these paper railroad companies had the audac-
ity to boast that he had spent over a quarter of a mil-
lion of dollars in bribing and corrupting the present
Legislature. The people have been plundered until
they are growing desperate, and there is real danger to our institutions. History teaches us that the
Roman emperors extorted money from their nobles and
fed their plunder to the rabble, but the Republican
party has just simply reversed this order by plundering the many to enrich a favored few. It is said that
anarchy and mob violence exist in the South, and that
the very existence of the government is threatened by
the Ku-Klux. How far these charges are true, it is not
for me to say, but I wish to call the attention of those
who prefer the accusations to the fact that the people
have been driven to desperation by an abuse of power
and a system of organized plunder that have, at least,
received the sanction of the government. Anarchy, or
a defiance of all authority, naturally follows despotism.
Tyranny is the father of anarchy, and there is a perpet-
ual conflict between the parent and offspring. Both
are evils, but so long as they successfully resist each

other their pernicious tendencies are checked, and the equilibrium of the government is maintained; but once this equilibrium is destroyed, all government vanishes. Russia has her mobs, but it is because the government is despotic.

"It is now five years since the clank of hostile sabres ceased, with the return of the victorious Northern soldiers to their homes, and, yet, the tread of the iron-heel of military despots is heard on our streets to-day. This military force is composed of mercenaries, hired in other States and brought here and equipped at the expense of this State, ostensibly to preserve the peace, but in reality to act as spies among our people and support the tottering fortunes of the Republican party. Sustained by such power, our Republican Legislature still continues the march of the State toward bankruptcy by making fraudulent appropriations and issuing bonds almost without limit. All this is done with a reckless disregard of public condemnation and private criticism. Honesty and capability are almost ignored as qualifications for positions of trust and responsibility, while under the reconstruction acts, thousands of competent and intelligent white men are denied any participation in the affairs of government, even the right of suffrage. The people of the State are fast drifting into three classes: office-holders, tax-gatherers and serfs.

"Finding myself out of sympathy with the policy and tendencies of the Republican party, I feel constrained to abandon it, and, therefore, I announce my intention to vote the Democratic ticket on election day in August next.

"I have only to say further, that having withdrawn

13

from the Republican party, I will not be a candidate
under its auspices for re-election to the office of judge
of this judicial district.

                          "RICHARD FARWELL."

Weston finished reading this card and uttered a
groan of disapproval.

"What do you think of it?" asked Tinklepaugh.

Weston was too much astonished to make an immediate reply, so Cross-eyed Telf, who was present, answered.

"I think the d—n scoundrel has turned traitor," said
that hideous looking, one-eared, cross-eyed barbarian;
"but I'll teach the fickle turncoat how to talk. I'll see
whether he votes the Democratic ticket at next election."   •

"But how can you prevent it?" asked Tinklepaugh.

"Why, I'll shackle his heels."

"I do not exactly understand you."

"Cage him, man; put him into bilboes."

"What for?"

"Why, for contempt of court."

"But, I must confess, I do not see how you can imprison him for contempt of court when he says nothing
about military courts in his card."

"Don't he call me a military despot, a mercenary
hireling, and a spy? And don't he say I imprisoned
and shot down citizens without authority of law or
right? I'll have the rebellious tyke boxed up in the
same room from which he took the young Ku-Klux
editor, before the sun sets this evening."

"That is right," said Weston, looking up from Judge

Farwell's card in the *Westville Conservative,* from which hitherto he had not been able to take his eyes since Tinklepaugh first handed him the paper. "There is nothing like insisting upon the proper respect for your authority, if you wish to maintain it, and the fact that such a supercilious article emanated from the pen of a Judge makes it all the more noticeable."

"That is true," said Tinklepaugh, "and such disparagement of Captain Tellefson's authority, coming from such an exalted source, has a tendency to aggravate the feeling of resistance to the established military rule now prevalent in the community. The Ku-Klux will want no better Shibboleth, under which to justify the preaching of their pernicious doctrines, than this text furnished by the renegade Judge."

"And I hope," said Weston, "that Captain Tellefson will not only imprison him, as he threatens, but hold him personally and criminally responsible for any riot or bloodshed his seditious article incites."

"Trust me to handle the renegade demagogue with a bridle and martingale," answered Cross-eyed Telf. "I'll soon have him under my thumb, and the first time he begins to champ the bit, or undertakes to kick over the traces, I'll turn him over to the tender mercy of Husky Diggs."

"And the parson," suggested Tinklepaugh.

"Yes, and to the merciful parson," answered Cross-eyed Telf, looking seemingly out of the window, but in reality closely at Tinklepaugh, and wondering whether that little scoundrel knew anything about the death of John Latham.

The reverend Dick Madison, though acting under

Cross-eyed Telf as half-servant and half-soldier, had been permitted to circulate considerably among his people on Sundays, in order to "fill his 'pintments," and the mention of his name in such a connection by Tinklepaugh caused Cross-eyed Telf to feel a little apprehensive, lest the long-tongued sermonizer had allowed his tongue to wag a little imprudently.

Having satisfied himself that Tinklepaugh knew nothing of the hanging of John Latham, Cross-eyed Telf announced his intention of leaving for the purpose of executing his threat against Judge Farwell, when Weston detained him.

"I esteem it a part of my official duty as the State's prosecuting attorney for this judicial district," began the designing little lawyer, "to invoke your aid in trying to punish the murderers of old Mr. Jasper Fontell. I have procured sufficient evidence to justify me in instituting a prosecution against several persons for that horrible crime, but the assassins are all members of Klan No. 40, and, since the Sheriff has so plainly evinced his sympathy with the Klan, I feel myself powerless to bring them to justice without the assistance of the military power, and I have therefore determined to ask you to help me."

"Nothing would tickle the blood in my veins quicker than to be able to nab a few dozen of the hell-hounds," answered Cross-eyed Telf, with a wicked leer. "Husky Diggs alone can muzzle a dozen of the cone-headed ghouls, and I'll warrant my force to bag the whole Klan if the order shall be given."

"Unless the Sheriff interferes in their behalf," said Tinklepaugh, as a mischievous smile played over his grimy countenance.

"D—n the Sheriff," answered Cross-eyed Telf, re-membering how that intrepid officer had outwitted him in the little bout at the court-house. "If ever I jostle against that rake-hell rapscallion again I'll settle the little account I have against him for the loss of my ear, and I intend to keep the wound green until I do meet him, too."

"Well, the encounter may take place soon enough to please you, if Weston insists on these prosecutions," said Tinklepaugh.

"And why not insist on prosecuting the midnight murderers?" asked Weston. "Do you think I can afford to sit idle and see the laws of the land set at defiance by a band of disguised assassins, and not raise a finger to stay the red hand of blood, simply because an arraignment of the butchers is likely to cause a riot?"

"Oh, no; I did not mean to say that you should refrain from a prosecution for any reason," answered Tinklepaugh. "I only thought to tease the Captain a little."

And yet Tinklepaugh was tortured with a vague apprehension that an indictment of innocent persons for the murder of Old Stingy Jap might lead to the detection of the guilty slayers.

"Well, I must confess that it does kinder stick a pin in my gizzard to tweak me about that little skirmish at the court-house," answered Cross-eyed Telf; "but I'll bet you next time I meet the Sheriff I'll have my spurs on, and he won't be allowed to snatch a bloodless victory, either."

"Well, I am going to furnish you an opportunity to

have another tussle with him," said Weston. "I propose to break up the Ku-Klux organization in this
community, at any cost."

"Just hand me your black list, then," said Cross
eyed Telf, "and I'll pnt an extinguisher upon the last
negro-whipping night-rider in the county."

Weston handed Cross-eyed Telf a complete list of
the names of all the members of Klan No. 40, which
included, of course, the names of those with whom
the reader is already acquainted.

No other writ, or warrant, for the arrest of the
alleged offenders was ever issued, but no other was
necessary in the estimation of the military satrap into
whose hands the "black list" was placed, and as for
Weston and Tinklepaugh, they both knew the innocence
of the persons thus accused in the drag-net catalogue,
but they had commenced to play a desperate game,
the final denouement of which demanded the violent
handling of their best trump cards, and the exciting of
the public mind having proven to be a trump card
device so far, they resolved to rely upon it the future.

Accordingly, next day a company of troops under
the immediate command of Husky Diggs was sent
out to make the arrests.

"Hello! old mouthy," said Husky Diggs, as he un-
ceremoniously entered the law office of Major Wyland
for the purpose of arresting him. "Cross-eyed Telf
sends his respects, and says he would like to see you
at the court-house."

"Tell Captain Tellefson that I transact all business
in my office, and if he has no business with me I do
not desire an interview," answered the dignified old
Blackstonian.

"Oh, don't jerk up your head so soon," answered Husky Diggs. "You'll have time enough to curl up your lip after old Cross-eyed Telf gits his foot on your neck, and cause enough too, I'm thinkin'; so don't go to bitin' your thumb yit."

"I do not understand such nonsensical jargon," said Major Wyland, "and as I have already signified my intention of declining the interview with Captain Tellefson at the court-house, you will please vacate the office."

"That's exactly what I'm goin' to do," answered the ruffian. "So jest come along without any further kickin'."

"What do you mean?" asked Major Wyland, rising and motioning to Husky Diggs to leave the room.

"Oh, I mean to vacate the office, as you told me," answered the shaggy-bearded scoundrel, advancing and taking Major Wyland by the arm. "Goin' to jug you, old man."

"You scurvey-faced villain," said the irascible old lawyer, shaking the viper from him; "surely you do not mean to arrest me?"

"That's exactly it," answered Husky Diggs.

"And by what right? Where is your warrant for my arrest?"

"Oh, I've got a *habis corpis* for you," answered Husky Diggs, with a sinister grin, remembering vaguely the conversation about that writ on the day Albert Seaton was rescued, but not comprehending its meaning. "Leastwise old Cross-eyed Telf said to bring your corpse, if you showed yourself too lively."

"I presume I might as well go with you to the trial,"

said Major Wyland, looking contemptuously around
upon the half-dozen ill-visaged ruffians accompanying
Husky Diggs.

"That's the right way to look at it," answered Husky
Diggs. "There is no use in takin' up cudgels against
a disadvantage; so jest put a wet blanket over your
mouth and prepare to tread the boards."

Major Wyland had no idea of any charge against
himself, and felt that there must be some mistake in
having him arrested, so he walked submissively to the
court-house by the side of Husky Diggs, feeling sure
of his acquittal, even before a court martial presided
over by Cross-eyed Telf.

"Make way for the old running-tongued speech-
ifyer!" exclaimed Husky Diggs, as he opened the door
of the large court-room upstairs in the courthouse, and
proceeded to shove Major Wyland in. "Old Talkative
is comin' in to lead the dance of the ghouls."

"But where is Captain Tellefson? And when is my
trial to take place?" asked Major Wyland, as he looked
around and saw that the capacious room was already
nearly filled with the members of the Klan.

"Cross-eyed Telf is down in the wine room samplin'
the kegs, I guess," answered Husky Diggs.

"But what about my trial?" again asked Major. "I
demand to be informed of the accusation against me,
and to have an immediate investigation of the charge,
as guaranteed in our State Constitution to all persons
arrested."

"Oh, go to hell with your Constitution and all other
sheep-skin books," answered Husky Diggs with a
wicked sneer. "Sich things are played out, old prat-

tle-mouth, and Cross-eyed Telf's hands are not tied by any sich brittle strings."

"You impudent, tyrannical devil!" exclaimed the infuriated old lawyer, and he attempted to strike Husky Diggs as he spoke, but that cunning demon was on the alert, and evaded the blow, and slamming the door in Major Wyland's face, locked him in.

Finding himself actually in prison, the irate old lawyer's cup of wrath boiled over. Judge Farwell was there, a prisoner, too, but his rage had somewhat subsided, and he came forward and vainly tried to console the aged captive.

"A prisoner, and at my age! Just think of it!" exclaimed the old man. "Here is the temple of justice prostituted into a prison by a hideous-looking, mercenary hireling, and innocent citizens incarcerated without indictment and without even being informed of the charge against them! The Constitution is set at defiance, and the laws trampled under foot by a petty tyrant! Liberty is dead, justice dethroned, law abolished, and personal security has been swept away by the coarse hand of a maudlin desperado! And this is 'Reconstruction' under the auspices of the Republican party!"

Several members of the Klan came forward to speak to him, but he was inconsolable, and sat for a long time on one of the long benches in the court-room with his face buried in his hands.

None of the prisoners had been given a trial, nor had they even been informed of the cause of their imprisonment, and Cross-eyed Telf was by this time too drunk to accord them a trial, even if he had been disposed to grant them that Constitutional privilege.

Sam Washburn was the only absent member of the Klan, and he had been spared only because he had not sufficiently recovered from the effects of his wound, received in the battle of a few days before.

The following is a sample yard of the bloody woof as woven by the before-mentioned outrage looms:

"MURDER BY THE KU–KLUX!

"THE MEMBERS OF A WHOLE KLAN ARRESTED!

"On yesterday Captain Crawford Tellefson, commander of the troops stationed at Westville, arrested and imprisoned every member of a den of Ku-Klux, known as Klan No. 40, for the murder of Mr. Jasper Fontell. Our readers will remember how the story of that horrible crime, which was published in these columns a few days ago, startled the whole civilized world, and caused the Governor of that State to proclaim West county in a state of insurrection, and put the county under martial law. Since that time Hon. Donald Weston, State Solicitor for that judicial district, has been unremitting in his efforts to ascertain who the perpetrators of the crime were, notwithstanding the fact that his own life was endangered by the investigation, and his labor in this direction has been rewarded at last by the accumulation of evidence amply sufficient to convict a whole Klan. Witnesses at first were timid, having been threatened with death, if they told anything, by the bloody-handed Ku-Klux; but as soon as the authority of Captain Tellefson had been firmly asserted and established, a feeling of security pervaded the county, and the witnesses were emboldened to tell the truth regardless of the menaces of the Klan. The evidence discloses a terrible state of lawlessness in that county. It shows that Mr. Fontell's death was agreed upon by the whole Klan, which makes every member guilty as an accessory before the fact, whether he actually participated in the hanging or not. The Klan includes persons in every class of society to be found in the Democratic party, which is fast becoming known in the South as the Ku-Klux party. It is said that one old lawyer, Major James Wyland, remonstrated vehemently against being imprisoned, but Captain Tellefson discharged his duty with an indomitable courage that is to be commended. There are other dens of the night-riding ghouls in the community, and an open war between them and the troops is daily expected. It is understood that the Governor has asked for the assistance of Federal troops, but if this aid is not furnished by the general government Captain Tellefson will be reinforced by other companies of State troops."

CHAPTER XVI.

A HEROINE APPEARS.

On the morning succeeding the incarceration of the members of Klan No. 40, a young lady appeared in the office usually occupied by the editor of the *Westville Conservative*, and, taking the vacant chair at the desk, sent the errand boy for the foreman. In answer to the call, a coatless young man appeared in the door, with his sleeves rolled up to his elbows, and his face, hands and arms besmeared with grease and rust from the printing presses.

"I have come to take charge of the editorial work here," said the young lady with a business-like air that evinced the stubborn determination of a very resolute woman.

The foreman, at first, had manifested some embarassment on account of his own untidy appearance, but now he was abashed by what he considered the impertinent usurpation of an obstinate woman. The young lady noticed his incertitude, and so attempted to dispel his perplexity by introducing · herself and asserting what, in her opinion, constituted her right to assume editorial control of the paper.

"I am Bessie DeVoy," she began (she had at once adopted her true name after the death of Mrs. Seaton), "and Albert, the editor, is my broth—," but the emotions excited by the last word stifled further utterance, and all her bold aspirations vanished, leaving her only a helpless, pitiable, grief-stricken girl.

The foreman now became convinced that his first estimate of her character was incorrect, and that, instead of the bold, resolute virago he had at first imagined her to be, she was evidently a poor demented girl, whose mind had lost its equilibrium on account of the disappointments and buffetings of a cold and heartless world, and who, hearing of the vacancy in the editorial department caused by the imprisonment of the editor, had fancied herself his divinely commissioned successor. Her beautiful face, gentle eyes, and quiet demeanor all negatived the idea of a shrew, and her deportment was inexplicable on any other hypothesis than that of mental aberration. But even this false impression was dispelled immediately on her recovery. She was only a woman, tender-hearted and emotional, and her agitation, under the circumstances, was perfectly natural, but she soon banished all excitation of feeling, and returned to her original resolution.

"You, doubtless, think me strangely agitated," she said, recovering her self-possession, "but you would not be surprised if you knew the circumstances that excite such feelings. It is altogether unnecessary, I hope, for me explain the cause of my embarrassment, and it will be sufficient for me to say that my intimate acquaintance with the editor of the *Conservative* will acquit me of the charge of intrusion, or usurpation, in taking possession of the editorial department. If you doubt that I am entitled to this privilege, you may become convinced by communicating with the editor. I presume the rigors of his imprisonment do not debar him from all communication with the outside world."

"I do not know what arbitrary rules the military

tyrant has established for the government of his prisoners," answered the foreman, who by this time was
convinced of the sanity of his visitor; "and, as for my
part, it makes but little difference who furnishes the
editorial matter, and I think our printers would be still
less disturbed by any idea of a change in this department, provided their weekly salaries are paid with reg-
ularity."

"I will allay all uneasiness on that account by paying them a week's wages in advance," said Bessie.
"What is the capacity of your force and printing
presses?"

"Our press has a capacity sufficient for the publication of a daily paper," answered the foreman; "but
our force of type-setters is able to produce only a
weekly edition."

"Can you obtain the additional help necessary to get
out a daily edition?"

"Very easily."

"Then ascertain what assistance is required, and procure it at once in order that we may begin the issue of
a daily to-morrow morning."

"And for what length of time shall I engage the additional help?"

"Make a contract for only fifteen days at present.
This will carry us over the election, and my purpose is
to publish a daily for campaign purposes."

The foreman looked at the delicate white hands and
pretty face before him, and wondered what influence
such an innocent creature could have in a campaign in
which race prejudice and unbridled party malignity
were the chief factors. The malevolence of party strife

was never more virulent, and the acrimonious debates heard on the hustings had to be reflected in the newspapers. Indeed, a paper that aspired to the dignity of being called the party organ, would be expected not only to reflect public sentiment, but would be required to take the initiative in all political movements, and to act as a sentinel on the walls. Hence, the shrewd foreman prophesied disaster to the enterprise in the hands of the unsophisticated girl; but the same mercenary motives he attributed to the other employees in the office, guided his own actions, and he was ready to embark in any undertaking that promised a continuation of his present employment.

"How many copies of the daily edition do you desire to have printed?" asked the foreman.

"I have not completed by estimate yet," answered Bessie. "I wish to have the paper furnished, gratis, to every person who can read in the county, until election day."

"That will entail a tremendous expense," suggested the foreman, still underrating the sagacity of the new editress.

"The work will be accomplished regardless of expense," answered Bessie, in a tone calculated to allay the suspicions of the penurious foreman.

"And how shall we secure the names and addresses of our would-be subscribers?"

"Go to the Sheriff," answered the girl, "and secure his assistance. He is well acquainted with the people of the county, and with the aid of his tax-books can give you the name and address of almost every person able to read in the county. He is an ardent Democrat,

and will readily assist you.   Take the county by town-
ships, and make the list as complete as possible.   With
the help of the Sheriff and your present subscription
list to the *Weekly Conservative,* I hope you will be able
to obtain a pretty accurate list for the daily.   Secure
at once the requisite number of employees, and then
revise your subscription book.   And remember we
have no time to lose."

Bessie laid a roll of manuscript containing editorial
matter on the editor's desk, and then placing a well-
filled purse in the hands of the foreman, left the office.

"By Jove!" exclaimed the foreman, as he gazed out
the window upon the queenly form retreating down
the street, after feasting his greedy eyes upon the contents of the purse; "that woman possesses business
qualifications that never fail.   At least, she has shrewdness enough to adopt a precaution that always secures
prompt action in this office.   I'll exhibit this purse to the
boys down stairs, and every mother's son of them will fall
in love with her without even seeing her face; though,
if I was a suitor for her hand, I would prefer that all
rivals should have their eyes dazzled by visions of her
gold rather than by a sight of her pretty face.   In fact,
I fear I should be as jealous as old Abraham was over
Sarah, and would call her my sister in order to avoid
the enmity of rivals.   Great God!" he exclaimed
again, after a few moments' reflection over the incident
of Abraham and Sarah before Pharoah, "I verily believe that girl is Albert Seaton's sweetheart, and she
tried to palm herself off on me as his sister in order to .
make some show of authority for assuming control of
the office.   I wouldn't be afraid to hazard this purse as

a wager that's it, and she choked at the word 'brother' because she couldn't tell a story. That explains her strange conduct at first; at least, I'll keep an open eye on her and find out."

"I wish to see Captain Tellefson," said Bessie, addressing Husky Diggs, as she appeared a few moments later at the door of the court-house.

"All right, ma'am," he answered with more civility than he had hitherto exhibited towards any visitor. "Jest keep still a minute, till I go an' tell him."

"There's a bundle of ruffles an' frills at the door what wants to speak to you," was the polite announcement the unlettered *aide-de-camp* made to his superior officer.

"Is she pretty?" asked Cross-eyed Telf.

"Purty as a pink," answered Husky Diggs; "an' she's pranked out in her Sunday bib and tucker, too."

"Tell her to come in, then."

Husky Diggs returned to where Bessie was left standing.

"The Capting's all smiles, Miss," he said, "an' says he'll be glad to see you, an' you needn't be too skittish, for you'll never know the squint-eyed loon is lookin' at you."

Saying this, Husky Diggs ushered Bessie into the presence of the tyrant, Tellefson, with all the obsequious deference he could command.

Cross-eyed Telf was sitting in front of a small table on which lay some writing material, and on the appearance of the young lady he arose and bowed politely. The side of his head from which his ear had been shot was turned toward Bessie, and the girl actually shuddered at his repulsive appearance.

14

"I have called, Captain Tellefson," said Bessie, "to inquire if I may be permitted to send a few copies of the *Westville Conservative* to your prisoners each morning?"

"Why, certainly," answered Cross-eyed Telf, looking, as Bessie thought, directly at Husky Diggs, and verifying that sage's prediction as to the uncertainty of the object of his master's vision. "But I thought the *Conservative* was only a weekly paper."

"It will be issued daily for a few weeks, at least," answered Bessie.

"Ahem!" said Cross-eyed Telf. "I had hoped the dirty sheet would be suppressed when we cooped the young Ku-Klux editor; but it seems that, as fast as we tie the thongs around the claws of one scribbler, another crops up to take his place."

"Just as many another deserving enterprise has been fostered by the hand of persecution," answered Bessie boldly.

"You are quite pert, Miss," answered the lop-eared clown, "but I'll have you to understand there is no persecution in this case, unless you call shackling the bloody hands of a murderer persecution."

"Albert Seaton is not a murderer," answered Bessie hotly, "and any insinuation to that effect is a malicious slander. But I do not desire to discuss that question now, and as I have accomplished the object of my mission, I wish to thank you for your kindness in granting my request, and now I am ready to return."

"I would like to know, before you leave, who the new quill-driver is to be," said Cross-eyed Telf.

"I expect to edit the paper myself," answered Bessie.

"O, ho! and there is to be a female band at the plough," answered Cross-eyed Telf. "Well, old Ben Butler said at New Orleans that 'there is no difference between a he-adder and a she-adder in their venom;' but I warn you now, Miss, that the first time you begin to sneer at my authority, you will find such a hornet's nest about your ears, you will wish you had never heard of a printing press."

"I shall conduct the paper according to my own notions of propriety," answered Bessie indignantly, "and in return, I warn you that you are preparing a halter for your own neck when you imprison innocent citizens, and refuse to accord them the Constitutional privilege of a speedy trial."

During the time consumed by this dialogue, Bessie had remained standing, having declined to accept a proffered chair, and she now turned and left the room, before Cross-eyed Telf could recover from his amazement at her defiance of his authority sufficiently to answer.

"Gosh! the ruffles, you spoke of, were in her temper instead of her skirts," said Cross-eyed Telf, to Husky Diggs after she had gone.

"She *is* a little cantankerous for sich a dapper gal," answered the witless underling; "an', then, you can't snap your fingers at a purty gal as easily as you can choke a Ku-Klux."

"Don't you put a thorn in your heart, and go into mourning on that account, until you see me deal with her," answered the ill-visaged master.

Bessie returned to her office in the *Conservative* building, where she found everything in a state of bustling activity. Her instructions to the foreman had been obeyed with promptitude, and every employee in the office, stimulated by the incentive found in the purse of gold exhibited by the foreman, had worked with such unremitting assiduity that the ponderous press was already rolling off the outside pages of the *Daily Conservative.* Every *attaché* of the office had been made acquainted with Bessie's alleged engagement to Albert Seaton, which the sagacious foreman had related to them, with many embellishments and improvements on the story of Abraham and Sarah as told in the twelfth and twentieth chapters of Genesis, and when she appeared in the door of the printing room, to observe how the work was progressing, a wave of excitement swept over the room, and all heads were turned toward the reputed betrothed, like heads of wheat all turn in one direction before a gust of wind. Bessie was altogether unconscious of the real cause of their curiosity, but attributed their excitement to their natural desire to see the successor to the imprisoned editor.

After satisfying herself that everything was moving on smoothly, and ascertaining that the editorial matter furnished by her early in the morning was amply sufficient to fill all available space in the first issue of the paper, she returned to the embrace of her dearest friend, Minnie Wyland, from whom she had separated that morning, after many earnest protestations on Minnie's part against her assuming the position of editress of a party organ, in a time of such turbulence and partisan violence.

It had been arranged that she should live with Minnie, at least until after the election, when everybody

hoped that the fever of political excitement would subside and the hand of persecution be stayed, and they
mutually endeavored to comfort and assist each other.
One of them mourned the banishment of a father and
an acknowledged lover, and the other bewailed the
absence of——well, no relation whatever; but her grief
was sincere and pathetic, notwithstanding.

Next morning the whole country was surprised at
the appearance of the *Daily Conservative*, but amazement changed to admiration when the announcement
was read that Judge Farwell was the Democratic candidate for Congress from that district, and Albert Seaton the county candidate for the Legislature. The
county was electrified, and letters and communications
approving the nominations came pouring in, until
there was not space for their publication. Every Democrat in the county rallied to the support of the stand-
ard-bearers, and the words " From prison to Congress "
and " From prison to Legislature " became the battle-
cries of the party.

The astonishment was nowhere greater than among
the prisoners in the court-house, when Husky Diggs
threw a bundle of papers in the door with the remark:

"Come an' git yer daily breakfast, an' the greediest
nose gits the most swill. Husky Diggs always feeds
his hogs the kind of slop they like to waller in best,
an' the little she-editor has b'iled ye some soup that
will tickle the nose of any swinish Ku-Klux. Come up,
an' git yer swill!"

The papers were eagerly seized and their contents
devoured with avidity, notwithstanding the heathenish
announcement of the ill-bred outlaw. It is impossible

to describe the sensations produced by the paper. Forty-eight hours of imprisonment had not tamed the spirits of the prisoners, but had increased their desire for a knowledge of what was going on in the outside world, wonderfully, and the article, proclaiming the candidacy of two of the prisoners, so thrilled their hearts that a shout of approval issued from a hundred throats at once and fairly shook the window panes.

Major Wyland advanced, his heart filled with emotion, and grasped the hand of Judge Farwell and Albert, and after congratulating them, assured them of his hope of their election. Every man in the house followed the example, and a regular scene of hand-shaking ensued.

CHAPTER XVII.

THE JUDICIARY EXHAUSTED.

Our late unfortunate civil war has frequently been spoken of as the "time that tried men's souls"; but, while conceding the fact that it requires great moral, as well as physical courage, to discharge efficiently the duties of a soldier, it must still be asserted, speaking with reference to the South, at least, that the real time that "tried men's *souls*" was the period of twenty years immediately succeeding the surrender at Appomattox. The unsettled condition of the country, resulting from the overthrow of the Confederate government, made the South an inviting field for political adventurers, and the conflict which then ensued between the right and the wrong, though noiseless, was more soul-destroying than the great war; because men, in their greed for wealth and inordinate desire for political preferment, forgot all moral obligations and resorted to crime in order to accomplish their aims and reach the goal of their ambition. Many, even among those who had reached the last round in the ladder and stood upon the very pinnacle of fame, prostituted their high offices to serve the basest of partisan purposes.

Human nature is a strange thing, and is unsusceptible of correct analization. Religious devotees will commit murder, or any other crime mentioned in the decalogue, if in their wild fanaticism they can be persuaded to believe that their crimes will further the interests of the church; and partisan enthusiasts will

do the same thing, in order to insure the success of
their party. Why this is so is incapable of explanation, and yet history teaches us the truth of such an
assertion. The history of the period of reconstruction
certainly justifies such a statement, as every person
who resided in the South during that eventful time
well knows.

The enterprising *Westville Conservative* may relate
how the Governor prostituted his powers to serve the
base conspiracy to perpetuate the reign of the Republican party, by denying to innocent prisoners their
Constitutional rights. The issue of July 25th, 1870,
said:

"Yesterday a writ of *habeas corpus*, issued by the
Chief Justice of our Supreme Court, was served on
Capt. Crawford Tellefson, commanding him to bring
the body of Major James Wyland before the Chief
Justice, that the cause of his imprisonment might be
inquired into; but the officer who served the writ
made return that Captain Tellefson indignantly refused
to surrender his prisoner, saying that he was acting
under the orders of the Governor in disobeying the
mandate, and that he would not give up his prisoner
until ordered to do so by the Governor, or compelled
to surrender to superior forces. He also intimated
that a court-martial had been appointed to try the
prisoners now confined in the court-house in Westville,
and sneeringly remarked that writs emanating from
our civil courts had 'played out.'

"On receipt of the Sheriff's return, the Chief Justice wrote to the Governor, inquiring whether Captain
Tellefson was acting under the Governor's orders in

disregarding⸗the writ, and on being informed that such was the⸗fact, the Chief Justice refused the order for an attachment against Captain Tellefson—a motion for an attachment having been made by counsel for Major Wyland—and the proceeding was dismissed.

"Thus the power of the Judiciary fails because our Governor, who is the Commander-in-Chief of the State militia, and has the whole power of the State at his back, elects to serve the behests of his party by trampling the Constitution under his feet. Innocent persons, men of high moral character and superior intelligence, are charged with the crime of murder, and held in close custody, and are denied the constitutional right of having the cause of their detention inquired into under the most sacred process of our civil courts.

"Verily, these are evil days, and our people are swallowing the very dregs of the cup of misery, but the *Conservative* would still advise the exercise of patience and endurance. Our affliction is indeed great, but a resort to violence would only aggravate the evil by producing civil war, and God knows our country has already seen enough of blood.

"For the action of our Chief Justice, there is at least a word of excuse; but for our Governor, none. Suppose the writ of attachment had been granted by our Chief Justice—who could execute it? The Governor has declared this county in a state of insurrection; he is the Commander-in-Chief of the State militia; every able-bodied man in the State belongs to the militia, and he has ordered a part of the militia to make these arrests and disregard the writs of our civil courts. How, then, could the Chief Justice order the remaining portion of the militia to violate the orders of their Commander-in-Chief, and engage in conflict with the portion already in the field? Thus it may be seen, that the whole responsibility for this subversion of the liberties and rights of our people, rests on the Governor, and the power of the Judiciary is exhausted."

CHAPTER XVIII.

A NEW SCHEME.

Dr. Wyland was a good man, whose faith in the right never deserted him; consequently he was not discouraged by the adverse decision of the Chief Justice, as recorded in the last chapter.

"God is not only good, but just," he muttered to himself, as he wended his way toward the courthouse on the morning after the announcement of the Chief Justice's decision, "and the right will yet prevail. Heaven knows these men are not murderers, and a prison is not the proper abode for such spirits as theirs."

So saying, he reached the courthouse, and was accosted by Husky Diggs.

"Hello! old pill-maker," said that worthy, as the good physician approached the door. "None of the jail-bird Ku-Klux is sick, so you needn't come prowlin' around tryin' to feel their pulses."

"I have not come to administer physic, as you imagine," answered the doctor, "but I simply desire to have an interview with my brother, Major Wyland."

"Have to see Old Cross-eyed Telf about that," answered Husky Diggs; "but I'll go an' ax him."

Cross-eyed Telf was found at his usual place beside a whiskey keg, but it was too early in the morning for him to be very drunk.

"There's an old leech at the door what wants to talk with the old cross-questioner," announced the bandit.

Having received the instruction from his master,

Husky Diggs ushered Dr. Wyland into the presence of the terror of the county.

Cross-eyed Telf was sitting beside a keg of his favorite brandy, and was too ill-mannered to rise on the approach of his visitor; and as he seemed to be looking directly out of the window, Dr. Wyland saw at once that he was likely to meet with a very cold reception. The squint-eyed worker of iniquity was more hideous looking than ever, for the gangrenous ulcer, that had appeared in the place of his lost ear, gave him a most frightful appearance.

"I wish to be allowed to speak with my brother, Major Wyland," said the doctor, addressing the repulsive looking being before him.

"And what do you want to see him about?" asked Cross-eyed Telf.

"I desire to consult him as to the best method of securing his release from prison," answered the doctor, boldly.

"Don't you know you have already tried your highest court, and made a flash in the pan?" asked the Cross-eyed bandit, looking savagely at the keg of brandy, as Dr. Wyland thought, but in reality at the doctor. "I tell you, old man, these bush-whacking Ku-Klux are to be tried by court martial, and no crafty old sheepskin-thumber can prevent it, so you just as well pocket the affront, and truckle to it at once."

"A trial before a court, organized for the express purpose of convicting, would be a farce," anwered the doctor.

"Not more so than the trial of a Ku-Klux before a Ku-Klux jury," answered Cross-eyed Telf.

" We have no Ku-Klux juries," answered Dr. Wyland;
" but, rather, with the aid of radical Sheriffs and
Judges, our juries are largely composed of scalawags,
carpet-baggers and negroes. But I do not care to discuss these matters now. I want to see my brother,
and to know if he can devise any means to secure his
release from imprisonment."

" I have already told you your civil courts were out
of date," said Crossed Telf; " but if you insist on
having the agile old limb of the law to whistle jigs to
a milestone, I'll send Husky Diggs after him and let
you see him bite the dust."

The case did look hopeless, indeed; but Dr. Wyland
had witnessed too many triumphs, due to his brother's
astuteness and skill as a lawyer, to abandon all hope
without giving the old lawyer a chance, and therefore
he insisted on seeing him.

Husky Diggs soon returned with his prisoner, and,
after an affectionate greeting, Dr. Wyland informed
his brother of the object of his visit.

" And on what ground did the Chief Justice refuse
to enforce the writ of *habeas corpus* by the issue of an
attachment? " asked Major Wyland, on being informed
of the previous failure.

" Because I told him such writs had played out,"
interposed Cross-eyed Telf.

" I have not seen a copy of his decision," answered
Dr. Wyland, " but I understand he based his opinion
on the ground that any officer whom he could appoint
to execute the writ, must necessarily be a member of
the State militia, and as the Governor, acting in the
capacity of Commander-in-Chief of the militia, had

already directed Captain Tellefson to disobey the writ, the authority of the Governor must be treated as paramount to that of the civil courts."

"That's it," again interposed Cross-eyed Telf. "I tell you, my sway in these parts is not to be sneezed at by any silk-gowned opinionator, and as long as I rule the roost the d—n Ku-Klux must keep in doors."

"Ah, I see the point," said Major Wyland, again leaving the boastful remarks of Cross-eyed Telf unnoticed. " The civil process failed, simply for the want of power to execute it."

"And is it true, then, that the power of our civil courts is exhausted?" asked Dr. Wyland.

"No," answered the lawyer, "that is never the case, except in time of war, and all we need now is to find a judge who knows his power and has the courage of his convictions."

"And where can we hope to find such a judge?" asked the doctor.

"Our Federal court judges would not be hampered by any such considerations as seemed to trouble the Chief Justice, and I recommend that you resort next to the judge of our Federal District," answered Major Wyland.

"Useless, I tell you; it is useless!" again ejaculated Cross-eyed Telf. "The Governor is my seconder, and as long as he backs me, I intend to hold you at the sword's point, though Grant himself should come to the rescue."

"I think I shall act on your suggestion at once, my brother," said Dr. Wyland, "and I will now take my leave of you, that no time may be lost." .

So saying Dr. Wyland departed, and as Husky Diggs conducted Major Wyland back to his quarters up stairs, old Cross-eyed Telf was heard to mutter:

"D—n that old needle-minded lawyer, I half believe the pawky old Ku-Klux will clip the wings of our plan yet."

"Hello! What fate is that you are bemoaning as if you had been steeped to the lips in misery!"

It was Tinklepaugh who spoke, as he and Weston entered the room. .

"Oh, I wasn't whining over anything," answered Cross-eyed Telf; "but I just thought to make a wry face at the old Ku-Klux lawyer."

"Come, now, no prevarication," said Weston. "That was not a tone of defiance we heard, so just confess that you are a little crestfallen over something."

"Oh, I was simply a crop too low, I guess," answered Cross-eyed Telf, "and was beginning to pipe my eye over nothing, so just join me in splicing the main brace with a bowl of grog."

Cross-eyed Telf handed a decanter of brandy to Weston.

"Come, gentlemen," said Weston, "I'll be the priest while we sacrifice at the shrine of Bacchus. Each man shall drain to the bottom the glass I fill for him."

So saying, he filled three glasses to the brim.

"Good! I vote you a silk surplice for your cleverness already," said Tinklepaugh, as he quaffed the contents of his glass.

"And I a silk skull-cap," said Cross-eyed Telf. "I see he don't undertake to help a lame dog over a stile with one hand. He said I was ailing, and I see he believes it, so I had just as well confess."

"Pray, what is it that troubles you, then?" asked Weston.

"Oh, nothing except that old Ku-Klux Wyland has advised his brother to apply to the Federal Court for another writ of *habeas corpus*," answered Cross-eyed Telf.

"And what are you going to do, if it is granted?" asked Tinklepaugh.

"Well, I'm only playing second fiddle in this matter, you know, and I reckon the best thing I can do is to hang on to the Governor's sleeve until the bubble bursts."

"You don't mean to suggest that we cannot depend on your assistance in this emergency, do you?" said Tinklepaugh.

"Depend on me?" answered Cross-eyed Telf, manifesting some displeasure at the question. "Didn't I tell you I was going to swing on to the Governor's sleeve as long as he stood at the helm? I'm no shilly-shally waverer, to play fast and loose with fortune, when the chances for me are all on one side. If the Governor flickers I fail, but as long as he sticks to me, I intend to torment the Ku-Klux until the last bloody night-rider crouches in the dust."

"That is a noble sentiment, fittingly declared," said Weston. "If the Governor possessed your pluck, I would entertain no fear of our success."

"And do you really apprehend that there is danger of our defeat?" asked Tinklepaugh.

"I feel compelled to answer that I do," said Weston. "If a Federal Judge should order a United States Marshal to execute the writ he would have the whole

Federal army at his back, and our State troops would be obliged to give way."

"But don't you know that the general government is with us in this fight against the Ku-Klux?" asked Tinklepaugh.

"Yes," answered Weston, "but there is the *habeas corpus* act of 1867, which our Federal Judges dare not ignore, and if a writ is once granted under the statute and placed in the hands of a United States Marshal, it would be enforced if, in order to do so, it should be necessary to call into requisition the whole power of the government."

"What do you think of our good Solicitor, now, Captain?" said Tinklepaugh, addressing Cross-eyed Telf. "It seems to me he is the one who is rather despondent, now."

"Yes, the thought of a United States Marshal seems to take all the grit out of his craw," answered Cross-eyed Telf. "He seems to be worse down-in-the-mouth than he accused me of being, when he first came in."

"Perhaps he needs another drink," suggested Tinklepaugh.

"I think I shall officiate at the altar, myself, this time." And Tinklepaugh imitated Weston by filling the glasses to the brim.

"I tell you what I would do, if I were a Federal Judge and an application was made to me to release the Ku-Klux prisoners," said Tinklepaugh, as he swallowed the fiery brandy. "I should treat them as having forfeited their citizenship when they joined an organization hostile to the government, and would leave them to the mercy of the State authorities."

15

" And that would be to hang the last one of them,"
said Cross-eyed Telf. " But I tell you what would save a
lot of hangings, even if we had the power to hang.
If we could muzzle the mouth of that little Ku-Klux
editress we would nip in the bud a sight of devilment
in these parts."

" I agree with you in that," said Weston. " Her suggestion of candidates for Congress and the Legislature
appears to have received a hearty response from the
Bourbon Democracy, probably because the men selected
were the most obnoxious to all other classes, and if
something is not done to check the popular drift they
will be successful at the polls."

" There he goes, again," said Tinklepaugh, " bemoaning our fate, instead up taking up cudgels and combat-
ting the opposing forces."

" And how can a man fight a young woman ?" asked
Weston. " If the editor was only a man, we could
have him horse-whipped and silenced in an hour, but
we cannot proceed in that way against a young lady."

" We might adopt the Captain's suggestion," said
Tinklepaugh ; " we might muzzle her."

" And how ? "

" Well," answered the wily ex-teacher, " suppose she
should conclude to abandon her work for a while, and
go to some summer resort for the benefit of her
health ? I know of a little hut—near the river, where
the murderous ghouls tried to drown me—that would
make a splendid watering place."

" That is a good idea ; but how can we induce her
to go ? "

" Oh, leave that matter to Captain Tellefson," answered Tinklepaugh. "He is an adept at kidnapping folks successfully, and leaving the memory of the deed only in a crazy brain."

Cross-eyed Telf was so startled at this last remark, that his eyes, which had never been properly set, fairly danced in their sockets. This was the second time Tinklepaugh had hinted that he possessed dangerous knowledge as to the manner of the untimely death of John Latham, but again Cross-eyed Telf remained silent, wisely thinking that if Tinklepaugh really knew anything, it could do no good to ask any questions.

"But would not the young editress be a little lonesome in such a secluded place all alone?" asked Weston. "How would it do to have Miss Minnie Wyland accompany her? If, by that means, we could drive her old father crazy, we would rid ourselves of our most dangerous enemy."

"That's a good idea," said Cross-eyed Telf. "Cage all the Ku-Klux and their offspring, and wipe them off the face of the earth forever."

Cross-eyed Telf was now thoroughly convinced that Tinklepaugh, as well as Weston, knew all about the death of John Latham, and the thought made him desperate.

"I have the plan, now," said Tinklepaugh, after a moment's reflection, aided in his devilment by the burning brandy. "I understand the young editress spends very little time in the office herself, merely sending the editorial matter down each morning. Now, if she could be removed to a place of safety before morning, what is to hinder us from preparing the editorial matter ourselves? But my plan is a little more extensive than that. Suppose we prepare an editorial, suggesting some plausible reason for withdrawing the candidacy of Judge Farwell and Albert Seaton, and leaving the Democratic party without candidates for these two important offices. You remember they were nominated solely by the *Westville Conservative*, and though the nomination has been generally acquiesced in by the party, yet they do not stand on the same footing of the other candidates, and a withdrawal of their names by that paper would throw the party into such a state of confusion that they would be unable to recover until after the election. It is now only a few days until the election, and the fraud could hardly be discovered in time to prevent its evil consequences."

"Your plan is an admirable one," said Weston, "and I believe it can be made successful if Captain Tellefson will agree to perform his part."

"Well, you have given me rather a ticklish card to play," said Cross-eyed Telf, " but you may always depend upon me to do the needful in any political job."

"That's right," said Tinklepaugh ; "and now there is only one other thing to do. We must see the Governor, and induce him, if possible, to protest against any interference on the part of the general government ; but if the writ should be issued, any way, then we must secure as long a delay as possible. Captain Tellefson must ask for time to prepare his return to the writ, and it may be that we can carry the matter over the election."

With this understanding the two little villains departed, leaving the lop-eared, cross-eyed villain to work out his own plan for accomplishing his part of the "political job."

CHAPTER XIX.

PRO BONO PUBLICO.

The diabolical ingenuity displayed by Weston and Tinklepaugh, in inventing the scheme for silencing the Democratic organ as detailed in the last chapter, was only equalled by the alacrity with which Cross-eyed Telf executed the plot.

Bessie DeVoy had worked so incessantly, since taking charge of the *Westville Conservative*, that the labor and excitement had already begun to prey upon her health, and Dr. Wyland, her physician and testamentary guardian, had recommended frequent exercise on horseback. Consequently, she and Minnie engaged in that delightful recreation every evening, accompanied by Uncle Ben, who had given up all hope of ever possessing " de forty acres an' de mule," and had returned to his old master's to live. The road selected was very quiet and secluded, leading along the river bank, and the young ladies enjoyed the exercise and had no fear of molestation.

On the evening after the plan for their abduction had been concocted by the three villains, and its execution determined upon as a political necessity, the two young ladies were riding quietly along the road, when all at once, on turning a sharp curve in the road following a bend in the river, they were confronted by a motley band of troops, some white and some colored, led by Husky Diggs.

" Hands up !" yelled the grim-visaged ruffian, adopt-

ing his usual method of making arrests. "You two
bundles of frippery, and the black escort, is my prisoners."

They were all three two badly frightened to make
any resistance; besides, any attempt at opposition would
have been useless. The reins of each horse were immediately seized by a couple of troopers, and the riders
were commanded to dismount.

"Oh, please do not kill us!" pleaded Bessie, recovering her self-possession sufficiently to speak, and recog-
nizing Husky Diggs as the man who had admitted her
to the interview with Cross-eyed Telf.

"Oh, don't git skeered, my butterfly," said Husky
Diggs. "We ain't goin' to hurt a hair on yer head,
nor a ruffle on yer skirt. Old Cross-eyed Telf jest
means to take ye under his pertectin' arm till the storm
blows over."

"Oh, please let us go," again pleaded the frightened
girl, made bolder by the reassuring words of Husky
Diggs. "I am sure we have done you no harm, and
do not deserve such treatment."

"Too late to plead innocent after bein' convicted,"
answered the heartless bandit in a tone that dispelled
all hope. "When petticoats are changed for breeches,
the wearer must expect to be served like a man.
Female politicianers must eat the bread in soak for
their Ku-Klux aiders."

These ominous words of the ruffian recalled to the
mind of the poor girl all the weight of the terrible responsibility she had assumed in taking charge of the
party organ—a thought she had been fighting back
with all her strength. For days her heart had been bur-

dened with a sense of responsibility she shuddered to contemplate, but her resolution had been fed and strengthened by the novelty and excitement of her position, and her power of endurance had been sustained thereby beyond her natural strength ; but now that her occupation was about to be rudely wrested from her, she realized for the first time the full gravity of her situation.

Husky Diggs was never dilatory in the execution of his master's orders, so, catching Bessie by both arms without further parley, he partly assisted and partly dragged her to the ground, and then performed a like service for Minnie. He next turned his attention to Uncle Ben.

"Git down, you nigger minion of a Ku-Klux master!" he shouted, in tones that brought to the poor negro's limbs all the suppleness they possessed in his youth, when he danced jigs in his master's kitchen, and caused his feet to strike the ground before his tormentor ceased speaking. "A purty servin'-man you are, to be settin' there in the saddle and the ladies waitin' to be led to their hotel."

The horses were now turned loose to go home as they pleased, and Husky Diggs conducted his newly made prisoners to the door of the little hut, designated by Tinklepaugh as a suitable place of safety for them. The building was a rude log structure, situated about a hundred yards from the river, at the foot of a small mountain. It was entirely surrounded by trees and a thick undergrowth of laurel, and the only means of access to it was by a little blind path, which wound among the trees and laurel bushes in such a labyrinthian maze as to bewilder any person not acquainted with its meanderings.

On reaching the door, both girls began to cry. The thought that this was to be their prison-house made the little frail hut look as formidable and dreadful, to them, as the great London tower appeared to the political victims of old England's persecutions in past centuries.

"Oh, I do not want to go in there," cried Minnie, shuddering and speaking for the first time since their seizure by the bandits. "Please let us go home. What have we done to incur the displeasure of any one? Why are we arrested and detained in this secret place?"

"Oh, come, now, Miss," answered Husky Diggs; "don't fly into a hysterical fit, now .No use to whine over spilt milk, you know, an' as to why you are here— all I know is, Old Cross-eyed Telf said for us to cage ye, an' that's enough. It ain't none of my business to ask questions, an' it won't do you any good to do so, neither; so jest step in an' make yerselves at home."

The girls feared to make any resistance, or to permit Uncle Ben to do so, and so they entered the house as directed. Notwithstanding the uninviting outside appearance of the little log hut, inside it was real cozy. The rough inside ceiling had been hastily covered with cheap wall paper; there was a neat little carpet on the floor, loosely laid, a lounge in one corner by the rude fireplace, a neat looking bed across the back end of the room, two chairs and a table in the middle of the floor, and on the table was a lamp and a basket, over which was thrown a white cloth.

Uncle Ben sat in the door without saying a word, and both girls sat on the lounge and cried.

" Oh, Minnie," said Bessie, clasping both arms around her neck and hugging her hysterically, " I alone am to blame for this, and, poor girl, you are made to suffer, too, for my foolishness. I ought to have known better than to have undertaken to edit a paper during such exciting times, and I remember you begged me not to assume such a task."

" Do not reproach yourself for anything on my account," answered Minnie. " Perhaps you did right in taking Albert's place; I am sure all will be right if ——."

Several *ifs* proposed themselves to Minnie's mind at the same time—one of them suggesting the contingency of their final deliverance unhurt; but that which choked her utterance, was one that was intended to introduce a clause in which the election of Bessie's candidate for Congress should be foretold. Not even the humiliation and peril she was then suffering could expel from her mind and heart the hope that Judge Farwell should be elected, and a reconciliation be effected between him and her father. Perhaps if she could have known that the imprisonment of the two men together had already caused them to clasp hands, in mutual friendship, she could have borne with less pain the thought of her confinement.

The sun soon hid itself behind the mountain, and the shades of a fateful evening began to gather and close around the little hut. Husky Diggs came in to light the lamp and announce supper, but the sight of the two weeping girls, lying prostrate on the lounge, clasped in each other's embrace, was enough to silence, for a moment, the tongue of even such a gibberish brute as he, so he silently emptied the rich viands in the basket on the table and retired.

Not even Uncle Ben had the courage or appetite to taste the food, so it was left untouched. All night long the two girls sat on the lounge and cried, and Uncle Ben sat in the door and watched and waited and nodded, hardly able to realize the situation, and utterly helpless to protect those under his charge. The troops remained outside the hut, and slept and watched by turns until day.

CHAPTER XX.

A LAST EFFORT.

Day dawned, at last, around the little hut in which Bessie and Minnie had spent a miserable night. The effulgent rays of the morning sun shot across the floor through the open door and peeped in at the only window in the walls of the little log building, and a whole colony of pretty birds, with sweet, chirping voices, gathered in the trees around and sang merrily the praises of the beautiful summer morning; but none of these brought comfort to the two sleepless, helpless, disconsolate girls within. Night, with its sombre hues and death-like stillness, is more in consonance with the feelings of newly-made prisoners than the open day, with its activity and life, because every evidence of the freedom without, when viewed through a prison window, is but a painful reminder to the captives within of the comforts of which they are deprived; so, the two girls still clung helplessly to each other, and even the merry chirping of the birds in the trees was a source of annoyance to them, notwithstanding this was the only sound they had heard since the evening before.

A negro can sleep in any climate, in any attitude, and under any circumstances. Indeed, it has been asserted, upon apparently good authority, that they have been known to sleep while actually following the plough; but whether this ancient implement of agriculture was guided with the same degree of skill under such cir-

cumstances is not recorded. Uncle Ben was no excep-
tion to the rule, and was sitting with his head resting
against the door-facing, drinking in the pleasant sunshine, when he was awakened by some one violently
shaking him by the shoulder.

"I hain't done nuffin' to be 'prisoned fur; I jes' lef'
de 'Publican party 'cause dey wouldn't gib me de forty
acres an' de mule," said Uncle Ben, rubbing his eyes.

The innocent old darkey had gone to sleep, under the
impression that all the troubles he and his *proteges*
were now experiencing were caused by his recent defection from the Republican party, on account of the
failure to carry out its pledges to its wards, the recently enfranchised negroes.

"Nobody cares about your party affiliations now,"
said Weston, for it was he who interrupted the man's
slumbers. "Just announce my presence to the young
ladies, and tell Miss Minnie I would like to have an interview with her."

Uncle Ben was a model servant, having received his
training in the days of slavery, and he announced Weston's appearance with the same ceremonious air he
would have adopted had he been announcing the presence of the most welcome visitor to the residence of
his late master. The young ladies, however, were too
much astonished at the approach of a visitor to evince
the same politeness; besides, they suspected that the
visit of the little Solicitor boded no good to them, so
they simply remained silent. But Weston had not expected a very cordial welcome, and so did not wait to
be invited in.

"Good morning, ladies," he said, taking a chair by

the table in the middle of the room. "I am sorry to see, from appearances, that you probably have not passed a very comfortable night."

"I would presume," answered Minnie, disengaging herself from Bessie's grasp and sitting upright on the lounge, "that whatever suffering we have had to endure is a matter of indifference to you, since I doubt not you are in a large measure responsible for it."

"You do me great injustice, I assure you," answered Weston. "I have already told you that I feel a deep concern in your welfare, and the purpose of my visit this morning is to reassure you of that fact."

"The most positive assurance you could give would be to release us from our present environments," answered Minnie.

"And that I have come to do," answered Weston, "but on one condition—that you well know."

"But what if I should refuse to accept freedom on such terms?"

"Then you must take the consequences."

"And what consequences are expected to follow?"

"I have only to say that I will not be responsible for them."

"But you will."

"Then if you prefer it, I will say that I will not attempt to prevent them."

"Mr. Weston," said Minnie, nerved to desperation by the very peril of her situation, "I told you once that I could never marry you, and I thought it was agreed then that your suit was not to be renewed."

"On the contrary," answered Weston, "I told you then that if I could not win your hand with the character for honesty, which I then possessed, I would renew my suit as the villain of villains, when considerations of personal safety would make it to your interest to marry me. That time has now come."

Minnie recalled the ominous threat, referred to by the unprincipled little scoundrel, and her whole frame shuddered with fear. But she did not hesitate.

"Mr. Weston," she said, with a voice quivering with emotion and fear, "I was taught at first to esteem you as a friend, but I find that your friendship is more deadly than your enmity. By your perfidy in misrepresenting Judge Farwell, you have forfeited all claim to my friendship, and having lost that, you cannot hope to have me regard you with the holier affection of love. Even the friendship I formerly professed and felt for you has been changed into a loathing hate by your insidious treachery and unscrupulous abuse of the power you possessed, and nothing now can ever change my estimate of your character, or induce me to entrust my happiness to your keeping. Death, accompanied with the most horrible agonies your diabolical ingenuity can inflict, would be far preferable to a conjugal union with one whom I view with such horror."

"Hold, rash woman!" shrieked the little demon in an impassioned voice, while his eyes gleamed with satanic fury. "Do not exasperate me and force me to execute my vengeance before the time. Let me keep cool, that the work may be accomplished with a hellish slowness of torture. Let me make the victims of my enmity cringe and cower before me, ere I inflict upon them the excruciating agonies of a two-fold death. To annihilate my enemies, without having them to bow before me in supplication, would be to rob myself of half the pleasure I would feel in their death. So, just keep cool, and let your final rejection of my suit, if such must be the outcome, be done deliberately; but I warn you now, that if such be your final decision (and I give you one more chance to save yourself and your friends), I will search the very archives of hell for a precedent for your punishment, and employ the craftiness of the devil himself in inventing new methods of torture. Every object of your affection shall rest under the ban of my malevolence, and I will pursue them to the death with scorpions of cruelty. Your love for my rival shall be a fang in your heart, and the very memory of him shall be a canker in your brain and a moth in your heart, that shall eat out every joyful recollection or pleasurable affection, and leave you the most bereft and wretched of human beings!"

" Go, then, and exhaust your inventions of cruelty," said Minnie, rising and stamping her delicate foot, while she pointed a well-tapered finger at the little villain before her. " I defy your power, though I know full well your desperate character. I have already told you I would prefer the most ignominious and horrible death to a union with you, and I tell you, again, I will never marry you as long as heaven furnishes me with the means of self-slaughter. Fire, water, poison, rope, steel, powder and lead, all the instruments of death, shall be exhausted before I will yield to such a calamitous fate!"

" Yes, a calamitous fate it would be, indeed," answered Weston, and the fury of his inordinate passion lit up his black eyes with an insane gleam. " But go,

marry the political renegade you call your betrothed,
and may all the curses of hell rest upon you!"

With these words Weston departed. He had been
foiled in every attempt to secure the hand of the girl
he loved so passionately, and with the malison last
uttered, he returned to Westville, where he was destined
to meet with another disappointment.

The *habeas corpus* cases, as advised by Major Wyland,
had been acted upon promptly by the Federal Court,
and the Court having found no just cause for the detention of the prisoners confined by Cross-eyed Telf, had
ordered that they be discharged immediately.

The result was as Weston had foretold. Even the
Governor was afraid of precipitating a war by advis-
ing resistance to the Federal authorities, so Cross-eyed
Telf was compelled to yield the custody of his prisoners to the United States Marshal, who released them
as ordered by the Court.

Weston was unaware of all this, however, when he
entered his room at the hotel, to find it already occupied by Tinklepaugh and Cross-eyed Telf, who had
been waiting for him.

"Hello! Lothario," said Tinklepaugh, as Weston
entered the room; "a nice fellow you are to be off
playing suitor to a young Ku-Klux pullet, while the
old cock-of-the-walk of the whole Klan is being turned
loose upon us again."

"What do you mean?" asked Weston, unable to
realize so many disappointments at once.

"Mean?" answered Cross-eyed Telf, with a wicked
leer, as his eyes began to chase each other as if each
was ashamed of the other's company. "Why he means

to say that the whole Klan of the ghouls have been uncaged, and our little game up, Just the day before the election, too."

"Yes," said Tinklepaugh, " the Federal Judge refused to listen to any appeal, even for a continuance, and the whole Klan has been turned loose on us on the very eve of the election."

" Well, if our scheme to defeat Judge Farwell and Albert Seaton succeeds, we will have accomplished something, at least," said Weston.

" I fear we are destined to be defeated in that, also," answered Tinklepaugh. "Our little trick has been discovered, and printers are already engaged in publishing a disclosure of the fraud."

" Then our whole game is up, indeed," said Weston, and he threw himself across his bed and groaned with rage.

16

CHAPTER XXI.

RESCUED.

"New goots! scheap goots! Hantherchifs, ribbins, fine dresses and jewelry. Come und puy vot I offers."

Such were the exclamations of an old, decrepit peddler, as he approached the little hut in which Bessie and Minnie were confined, soon after Weston left.

The old man wore a long gray beard which, with his long, flowing white hair, left little of his swarthy face exposed to the gaze of the curious, and, though a little corpulent for one accustomed to the hardships of a peddler's life, he was bowed with age and walked with a complaining limp. He had on a long linen coat, or duster, much the worse for wear, and which, owing to his stooping posture, almost touched the ground as he hobbled along. His pants were made of homespun flax, and though they appeared torn and threadbare in places, they still retained their primitive yellow color, owing doubtless to the fact that they had not been washed often enough to turn white. His shoes, also, were old and yellow for the want of polishing, and were turned up at the toe.

He spread his wares out on the ground in front of the door, and continued to invite purchasers to come forward and buy, without success, until Huskey Diggs, remembering the instruction given him not to allow any person to approach the hut, came up and ordered him to leave.

"Out from here, you lickpenny landloper!" shouted

Husky Diggs, in a voice that threw the harmless old peddler into a state of terror " Military commissaries is no place for vagrants, so jest bundle up your duds an' git, an' don't bother our ears with no more of your furrin-tongued gibberish."

Thus admonished, the hapless old pedestrian repacked his goods with a trembling hand, and, without further parley, was soon hobbling back along the narrow path leading out into the public road.

Once in the road, he turned in the direction of West-ville, and notwithstanding his apparent age and feeble-ness, he made such fast progress that he was soon in the midst of the town.

"I thought I would find them," he muttered to him-self, as he entered a well furnished room and threw off his disguise. "Old Cross-eyed Telf thinks he is mighty sharp, but I'll pay him yet for this wound in my breast."

It was Sam Washburn, the spy of the Klan. He had recovered from the effects of the wound, he received in the battle at the court-house, sufficiently to resume his work, and his labors had just been rewarded by the discovery of the only prisoners left in the custody of the tyrant, Cross-eyed Telf.

His next duty was to inform the friends of the young ladies of the place of their confinement, and this he did immediately. In an incredibly short time, more than a hundred well-armed young men were galloping to-ward the little log prison by the river, swearing veng-eance against Cross-eyed Telf and all the mercenaries under him. Most of them had just been released from prison themselves, and, while the main object of their haste was to rescue those still imprisoned, they were equally anxious for the opportunity of wreaking their vengeance against their lawless persecutors and retaliating for some of their acts of needless cruelty. Maj. Wyland, Judge Farwell and Albert were in the crowd, and no horses were fleeter footed than those rode by them.

No concerted plan had been agreed upon for the rescue of the prisoners, owing to the great hurry and confusion, and the first warning given Husky Diggs and his men of the approach of the party of rescuers was furnished by a volley of balls, one of which pierced the breast of the villain named and sent him rolling in agony upon the ground.

The next moment Maj. Wyland rushed forward and seized Minnie in his arms. The poor girl had mistaken the cause of the alarm, and, imagining the firing came from Weston and his allies who had returned to execute the threat made that morning by the rejected little Solicitor, she had fainted and fallen prostrate on the floor.

"Oh, my darling child!" cried Major Wyland, as he kissed her and pressed her to his breast. "They have murdered you, at last, and have left me alone just as I thought to have you with me again. Oh, my idol, my poor daughter!"

Others, seeing Minnie's condition, took charge of her, and placing her again on the floor, soon restored her to consciousness.

Bessie, though excited, was less frightened, and stood up to meet her liberators as the ideal little heroine she had been during all these days of peril. Hers was one of those quiet, strong natures that never quail before any danger, nor succumb to any foe.

Albert was proud of her, and as he imprinted a kiss on her flushed cheek, his eyes beamed with genuine delight; but whether the kiss was an expression of brotherly affection, or another attempt to imitate old Abraham by trying to palm off his sweetheart before the public as his sister, not even the sagacious foreman in the *Westville Conservative* office could have told with certainty. Probably Albert himself could not have told how it was, but his joy was supreme, nevertheless, and so it was with Bessie.

After the most cordial greetings and hearty congratulations all round, they returned to town, leaving the military hirelings to bury the lifeless body of Husky Diggs, or convey it to their brutal master, as they saw fit.

As the crowd rode by the Midland hotel, conveying Bessie and Minnie to the house of their friends, Weston and Tinklepaugh, looked out from the windows of their rooms with a fearful scowl on their faces. There were more than one hundred votes in that crowd, and tomorrow each ballot would fall into the box like clods upon a coffin, sounding the death-knell of all the hopes that had stirred the breasts of the two little scoundrels since the death of Old Stingy Jap.

That evening, as Judge Farwell and Minnie stood by a large window in the parlor of Major Wyland's residence, talking over their recent adventures and misfortunes, the venerable old lawyer approached them, and taking Judge Farwell by the hand, he placed his other arm around Minnie's neck, and, stooping down, kissed her tenderly and lovingly.

"I have been very cruel to you both," he said, as the tears coursed down his cheeks, and he seemed almost choked with emotion; "but I see my error, now, and have repented it, and now come to ask your forgiveness. You have my consent to marry now as soon as you please, and shall have my blessing, also. God bless you both and prosper you! You have been a good girl, Minnie," he continued, kissing away the tears that rolled down her cheeks, "and I honor and commend you for observing my wishes, notwithstanding my conduct toward you was cruel. I assure you I will never more interfere to deprive you of one moment's happiness. Again I say, God bless you both!" and he turned and left them alone in their happiness.

CHAPTER XXII.

THE ELECTION.

The morning of election day dawned brightly, and as the first streaks of light shot across the fields, they were followed in every direction by men in eager haste to be first at the polls in the different precincts. The polls opened with the rising sun, the first effulgent rays of which lit up a sea of eager faces at every voting place. All classes were there, represented by all colors, degrees of intelligence, shades of opinion, and all political organizations. The old "Unioner," commonly denominated a scalawag, argued with the Democratic neighbor and charged the Democratic party with "bringing on the war;" the imported statesman from the North, commonly called a carpetbagger, elbowed his odoriferous "brother in black" and again deceived him into voting the Republican ticket, with promises of "de forty acres an' a mule;" the Ku-Klux jostled against the Union Leaguer and shoved and pushed for a place at the polls; and the gray-haired veteran of the Confederacy, representing the most intelligent class of all, but not allowed to vote on account of the inhibition contained in the Iron-Clad Oath, stood and gazed upon the motley throng and wondered whether this really was "the greatest government on earth."

Early in the day Judge Farwell went forward and redeemed his promise to vote the Democratic ticket, and many other former Republicans, disgusted with the meanness of their party, marched up and did like-

wise. The result is easily foretold. The Democratic
ticket was overwhelmingly elected throughout the
State, and the gigantic system of public plunder, inaug-
urated by the Republican party, began to totter and
fall. The glorious sunlight of Hope began to pierce
through the mists, that had remained so long settled
over the quagmires of hate, and soon the clouds rifted
and drifted away.

Bessie and Minnie remained up that night to hear
the election news, each anxious for the success of her
particular candidate. There was a full moon, and its
rays fell gently upon the forms of the two pretty girls
as they stood in the broad piazza, watching and waiting for Judge Farwell and Albert, who had promised
to come down and give them the news as soon as the
reports were all in.

About twelve o'clock, the two young men entered
the gate and started up the graveled walk toward the
house; but Bessie was too anxious to wait for their approach, and rushed forward to meet them, exclaiming:

" Oh, it is good news, I know; I can tell from the
smile on your faces, even in the moonlight!"

" Yes, it is good news," answered Albert, taking her
hand in his, while Judge Farwell walked on to the
house. " The whole ticket is elected by an overwhelm-
ing majority."

"And that includes you, of course," she answered,
while her eyes beamed with delight.

" Yes," said Albert, leading her into the soft shadow
of a magnificent magnolia, "and I am indebted to you
for even the suggestion of my name as a candidate. I
feel now that an honorable career has opened before
me, and I will walk in it if ——"

"If what?" she asked.

"If you will help me," he answered, taking both her hands in his and pressing them to his lips. "Will you help me, Bessie, to make my life honorable and successful as you have started it? Since you cannot be a sister to me, will you be my wife?"

And she answered softly, "Yes," but only Albert and the magnolia heard, for Judge Farwell and Minnie were already busy planning their wedding tour, which was to end at Washington, at the beginning of the session during which Judge Farwell was to hold his seat in Congress.

Where novelty ends in a novel there the novel itself should end. Both the love stories having been traced to a successful termination, it now only remains to dispose of the different characters in a summary way, and the little book will end.

Old Major Wyland lived only a few years longer to repent of his former opposition to the marriage of Minnie and Judge Farwell, but he made a complete atonement at last, at least in the eyes of the world, by dying and leaving them a princely estate.

Uncle Ben lived on, as the trusted servant of the house, a few years after the death of his late master, and then died, uttering with his last breath the only complaint that his freedom as a citizen had ever known, that "de 'Publican party done fooled de niggers erbout de forty acres an' de mule."

Mrs. Latham recovered her sanity and memory, too,

to such a degree that her testimony, with the aid of that of Rev. Dick Madison, who turned State's evidence to save his own neck, was sufficient to convict Cross-eyed Telf of the murder of her son.

Cross-eyed Telf, as has just been intimated, was convicted of the murder of John Latham, and was sentenced to be hung, but the sentence was commuted to imprisonment for life, and he afterwards escaped under the amnesty act.

Dick Madison, having turned traitor against Cross-eyed Telf, sustained his new character by betraying Tinklepaugh for the murder of Old Stingy Jap, and Tinklepaugh was convicted and sentenced to be hung, too, but had his sentence commuted with that of Cross-eyed Telf, and after the passage of the general amnesty act he was pardoned.

Weston, though the real instigator of a majority of the crimes committed in the community, and equally guilty as Tinklepaugh, managed always to keep out of court, after being defeated for the Solicitorship, and as Tinklepaugh refused to imitate Dick Madison by turning State's witness against Weston, he was allowed to join the exodus of carpet-baggers that began immediately after the election, and return to his native State. The bonds he and Tinklepaugh stole from Old Stingy Jap, after murdering him, were repudiated by the Legislature, of which Albert Seaton became an honored member, and became utterly worthless. He never returned to execute his threats against Minnie and her friends, and she and the Judge still live unmolested.

Bessie and Albert still live at the old Seaton homestead, and twenty-three years of their happy married life has already vindicated the wisdom of their parents in betrothing them in their infancy by will.

After the restoration of peace and harmony the Klan disbanded, but many a citizen of Westville still remembers with gratitude the services of Ku-Klux-Klan No. 40.

THE END.

www.ingramcontent.com/pod-product-compliance
Lightning Source LLC
Chambersburg PA
CBHW031400020726
47499CB00005B/1462